BRUTAL
FORTRESS

Also by L. Penelope

Earthsinger Chronicles

Song of Blood & Stone

Breath of Dust & Dawn

Whispers of Shadow & Flame

Hush of Storm & Sorrow

Cry of Metal & Bone

Echoes of Ash & Tears

Requiem of Silence

The Eternal Flame Series

Angelborn

Angelfall

Other Romance

The Cupid Guild Complete Collection

Writing As Leslye Penelope

The Monsters We Defy

Daughter of the Merciful Deep

BOOK THREE OF THE GLASS WARS

BRUTAL
FORTRESS

L. PENELOPE

HEARTSPELL

Heartspell Media, LLC

ISBN: 978-1-944744-31-1 (eBook)

ISBN: 978-1-944744-32-8 (trade paperback 1)

ISNB: 978-1-944744-33-5 (trade paperback 2)

Copyeditor: Sydnee Thompson

Cover design: James T. Egan of Bookfly Design

The Story So Far...

In *Savage City*, Talia Dubroca is transported from her deathbed in our world to Aurum, a post-apocalyptic city that is an alternate world's version of San Francisco. Here, two shifter clans are locked in war: the Nimali, who change into animals that match the form of the daimon spirits they harness, and the Fai, who also link with daimons but keep their human forms while wielding animal abilities. Talia is saved from an attack by the monstrous Revokers outside the city's wall and healed of their lethal venom by Ryin Arinson, a Fai healer and prisoner of war.

Talia is mistaken for the missing princess of the Nimali, Celena. Prince Shad, Celena's stepbrother, advises her to continue the ruse, as outsiders do not survive among the Nimali. Talia is opposed to the plan until she meets King Lyall, who believes she is his daughter and has lost her memory. Faced with the loving father she's never had and the adoration of the people, she agrees to the charade until Shad can find a way to send her home.

Lyall assigns Ryin to shadow Talia in case she requires more healing, and she is horrified to discover that the Fai prisoners are essentially slaves, with their souls being held hostage.

Talia vows to use her position as princess to improve things. However, she struggles with the unfamiliar rules of Nimali society and is convinced that Lady Dominga, the princess's best friend, is suspicious of her.

Over time, Ryin and Talia fall for one another. They learn that Revokers are being experimented on in a lab in the Citadel—the Nimali stronghold—and their venom synthesized into a chemical weapon that Lyall plans to use to eradicate the Fai. With the enemy gone, the Nimali will have unfettered access to the Fai's untapped bliss matrices, as their own sources of power are fast becoming depleted.

Ryin discovers the keys to Fai freedom, their stolen souls, are being kept in the vault that Talia has access to. Together, they free the Fai prisoners, who then face the Nimali army in order to escape. Von, a Fai rebel, captures Talia, wanting to use the "princess" as leverage to aid their retreat, but Dominga reveals the truth: that Talia is just a pretender.

When Shad defies Lyall, the king shifts into his dragon form and burns the man badly. Meanwhile, the Revokers escape from the lab and attack. Nimali and Fai fight together to defeat them, and Talia undergoes the ceremony to gain a dragon daimon before shifting for the first time. Ryin is apparently killed, but revived by his phoenix daimon.

King Lyall dies in the battle after rushing to protect Talia because of her resemblance to Celena. Before leaving the Citadel, Ryin heals Prince Shad's injuries, trusting that he will be a more just king and deal more fairly with the Fai. Ryin and Talia head off for the Fai lands, unsure of her reception as a dragon shifter.

In *Beastly Kingdom*, Shad is now king of the Nimali. While he faces opposition from those who don't believe he is up to the task because he didn't kill the former king, Shad believes that

Princess Celena's return and their subsequent marriage will legitimize his rule. He has sent a trusted soldier to search for the missing woman.

Against the advice of his councilors, Shad attends a peace summit with the Fai. Their leaders propose a marriage contract between the two clans to avert a prophesied mutual destruction. Knowing his daimon would never accept a Fai partner, Shad agrees to a thirty-day betrothal with Xipporah, a Fai warrior, to buy him time to negotiate a true peace treaty.

On the way back to the Citadel, Shad and Xipporah's caravan is attacked. They're taken captive by a human group claiming to have saved them from their true attackers and wanting to trade information for food and supplies. Xipporah is surprised that Shad shows mercy and considers the humans' request. She is not eager to spend a month with her enemy, but she has been given a secret mission to determine whether the Nimali really destroyed the Revoker weapon they developed or still plan to use it to annihilate the Fai.

The bliss cells in the Citadel are being sabotaged, and the critically low levels of bliss result in the rationing of food and power. Xipporah reluctantly agrees to use her tiger daimon's abilities to boost production in the indoor farms. There, she discovers the Fai rebel Von has been hiding in the territory and is responsible for the sabotage. He is also moving forward with a plan to attack the Nimali from within, but the civilian casualties are unacceptable to Xipporah.

Shad and Xipporah grow closer, each shedding their preconceived notions of the other. Xipporah discovers she can recharge the bliss but fears what it would mean if this knowledge were widely known.

She finds the chemical weapon that Shad believes had been destroyed but she quickly realizes Von is planning to use it on the Nimali populace. She alerts Shad, however, both of them are arrested in a coup by Shad's enemies.

Those loyal to Shad break them out of prison, and

Xipporah heads for Fai territory to warn them about the attack and the coup leader's plan. However, she's kidnapped by a human faction who had attacked them.

Shad rescues her and, assisted by human allies, they prepare to retake the Citadel. However, Von has activated an explosive device laced with poison inside the building and it cannot be defused.

The rush is on to evacuate everyone, and Xipporah uses her power to recharge the bliss and assist.

Fai backup arrives and creates a magical barrier to contain the effects of the lethal explosion and prevent it from destroying the homes of both clans. Then, a call for help comes from the wall.

Princess Celena has returned with an army of Revokers at her back.

Prologue

Celena

THE DISTANT ROAR of a dragon reverberates across the broken shell of the city. The hair on the back of my neck rises, though the danger is far from here. Still, a predator roams the night. With no claws, no fangs, no venom or fire, I am powerless against it. The only thing protecting me is the fact that the most dangerous creature in this city is my own father. And he would never harm me.

At least, that's what he says.

Now is the perfect time to go, with him distracted and engaged elsewhere. I focus on the water lapping against the rocky sand of the shore, licking at my boots. The old bridge, with its rusted struts poking out of the water like giant fingers, rises in the distance, limned by moonlight. If it were intact, my task would be easier. Of course, if it were intact, the Revokers would have crossed it and overrun the city years ago.

They cannot cross water. This has always protected us, being surrounded on three sides by the ocean and the bay. The wall to the south is our last defense, since the terrifying beasts cannot go underground, either. But these protections make the world outside the wall impossible for every soul in Aurum. And outside is exactly where I need to be.

Footsteps crunch on the gravel behind me. The only thing surprising about them is that they took this long to materialize. I didn't tell her that tonight was the night I planned to leave, but somehow, she knew anyway.

I turn away from the mesmerizing waters to face her. The moon's glow illuminates her dark, sharp features.

"So, you're really doing this?" she says.

"Yes. It's my only option."

She snorts. "It is *not* your only option. It's just the one you're choosing."

I cross my arms, matching her defensive position, tired of this debate. "Father is keen to have me do the trial again. It needs to be on my own terms this time."

One year ago, I underwent my first trial for a daimon. A little late as far as these things go—most do it by the age of twenty-one. But I procrastinated, perhaps to my detriment. Would it have mattered if I had done it earlier? Tried at eighteen, like some of the Umbers? Like Shad, my stepbrother, who leashed a powerful dragon?

I take a deep breath and gaze at the peaceful ripples of black water shot through with the moon's pale glare. You'd never know that all around the placid loveliness of this sight is destruction. "I don't want to fight, Dominga. I don't want to have this conversation at all. This is what I need to do. I know it, I *feel* it."

"Well, you're doing a poor job of hiding your tracks," she says snippily.

I look over, and she holds up a scrap of fabric from where I snagged the hem of my coat. It happened as I was sneaking out of the Citadel, having ducked my assigned guards. I'd gotten caught on a jagged bit of metal sticking out of the foundation of an unreclaimed building. Knowing the patrols were getting closer, I'd pulled away in haste.

She pockets the fabric and clucks her tongue. "Go over the plan again." When I start to protest, she raises a hand. "I know we've been over it a hundred times, but for my peace of mind."

I take a deep breath, knowing that I owe her this. Her concern isn't misplaced. What I'm attempting is dangerous. But staying to do my trials here, facing another failure, is just as risky. Eventually, it will be deadly.

Nearby, a knotted snarl of bristly bushes springs from the cracked concrete of a pre-Sorrows dock. Hidden amid its tangles is a small boat used by the Fai drudges. Apparently, they trawl for seaweed, using it to supplement their diets. My skin crawls at the notion, then I shiver again at the plight of the men and women my father has chosen to indenture— enslave, in reality. They are prisoners of war in our long conflict with their clan. I don't begrudge them their odd prac- tices, even if I don't understand them. I only hope that the loss of this boat will not be felt too acutely.

"I will use the boat to cross the bay and locate the bliss pool my mother spoke of. The one where she did her own trial. Out of an overabundance of caution, I've packed a month's worth of supplies." I point to the pack on my back. "And I have her tablet with all her vids to me on them. They have everything I'll need."

In the twelve years since my mother Rada died, I'd watched her vids probably hundreds of times. They were her gift to me, recorded once she knew she was sick with an illness that even the imprisoned Fai healers could only keep at bay for so long.

In her messages, she told me how she had failed her trials twice, losing her shadow and voice souls in the process. But as a child, her grandmother's tales had enraptured her. The older woman had told of bliss pools in other parts of the land, places the Nimali had access to before the Sorrows, before the world broke apart, and most humans died, and the shifters took over Aurum. Before the Revokers appeared and we built the wall that cages us on this peninsula.

A third failure in the trials means death, as a person can live without two souls but not without three, and Mother wanted to live. So she and a childhood friend crossed the water on a raft they built. And it worked. She found a pool of bliss untouched for decades, leashed a powerful daimon, and became queen. Exactly what I'm going to do.

Dominga purses her lips. "There are so many ways it could go wrong. That bliss pool she spoke of may not be accessible any longer. It may have dried up."

"Dried up?" I scoff. "When has that ever happened? There are no Nimali there, nor Fai, to use it. And humans don't even know about bliss."

"You have no idea who or what is over there." Her voice is icy.

"Our air patrols monitor the eastern city periodically. There is nothing there but miserable humans and Revokers."

"Exactly!" she says triumphantly.

"My mother avoided them. If I stick to the waterways and the tunnels, places they can't go, then I'll be safe. There's only a short distance over land that I have to travel. I can do it quickly. Stay quiet and nimble." My eyes plead with her. "I have to try."

Dominga leashed a predator daimon on the first attempt. She has no idea what it feels like to fail, especially with such high expectations on me. It's not power that I want. Being princess of the Nimali does come with privilege, but that means nothing to me. It's the responsibility I seek. My father's rule is harsh. When I am queen, I can enact change. Do things differently. "You will become the queen who is needed," my mother said. But only if I leash a dragon. It is the only way I have any hope of helping my people.

My best friend looks ready to argue more, but the sound of approaching footsteps makes her snap her lips shut.

The patrol is here.

I had planned to be gone before they swept this area. Dominga's arrival put me behind. My jaw tenses and I stare at her.

If she really wants to prevent me from leaving, all she has to do is alert them to my presence. I may be the princess and hold authority over just about any Nimali—I could force them to turn the other way and leave me about my business—but they would face my father's wrath when my disappearance is discovered. And his wrath is deadly.

With a last pleading look at Dominga, I slip silently behind the bushes that hide the boat. She remains out in the open, in full view of the soldiers turning the corner in lockstep. I hold my breath.

A black-clad female soldier marches next to a prowling lioness. Both stop short when they spot Dominga.

"My lady, are you all right?" the woman asks as the lioness scents the air.

Every muscle in my body tenses as I wonder whether the big cat will perceive me. Part of my months of preparation was to sponsor the research of an olfactory scientist developing a perfume that masks scents. Useful for hiding ourselves from our Fai enemies, but I had another purpose in mind. I'd sprayed myself with an early prototype before leaving the Citadel, and now I desperately hope it works. Otherwise, the lioness will sniff me out in moments.

"I am perfectly well," Dominga replies, nose in the air. "I have business here."

The soldier looks around dubiously, her thoughts plain on her face. What business could a powerful Cardinal, the daughter of a member of the king's Council, no less, have on the deserted shores of the bay so far from the center of Nimali society? However, understanding her rank, she voices none of this aloud.

"Would you like us to stay and escort you back to the Citadel, Lady Dominga?" the soldier asks, tentative.

"No. Complete your duties. I am perfectly capable of taking care of myself." She takes full advantage of her reputation for imperiousness and waves them away.

The lioness's nose crinkles, nostrils flaring, as intelligent, golden eyes scan the area, seeing much more than any human can in the darkness. I will my body into stillness. My lungs burn, needing a breath, but I continue to deny them.

Then the cat looks away. The soldier in her human form nods respectfully at Dominga and the two continue on their patrol. One pair of boots and four paws pad off down the shore.

I wait as long as I can before sucking in a ragged breath. "Thank you," I whisper, my voice barely audible across the distance that separates us. But she hears.

Her eyes narrow. "Your plan had better work, Celena."

A frisson of fear ripples across my skin, raising goosebumps. Every aspect of my plan has been checked and double-checked. I know the content of my mother's vids well enough to recite them by heart. I am as ready as I can be.

"When I return, I will have a dragon daimon and I will be queen. Mark my words."

Though I'm still crouched behind the bush, Dominga's gaze arrows directly to me. She nods once, then turns away.

When her footsteps disappear completely, I push the boat into the calm waters of the bay, ignoring the icy prickle of alarm clinging to my skin.

ONE

Victor

THE FIRST TIME I DIED, I fell flat on my back on the basketball court near my house, staring at a single bird circling high in the sky. Wondered if it was a vulture and if it was going to swoop down to pick at my bones. Drink up the blood streaming out of me and pooling on the cracked asphalt. People were running and screaming all around me, and I knew I was dying.

I thought at least I'd get to see my sister again.

Shaking off the regret and old grief, I yank myself out of the mood hanging over me, thick as the endless fog. Now, I'm the only thing in the sky, finishing my morning circuit of the city, flapping my enormous bat-like wings and gliding toward home. There aren't many birds left, at least not around here. Certainly no vultures—the monsters don't leave anything for them to feed on.

On clear days, though, I'll catch glimpses of flocks of small creatures flying in formation far to the east of the city. Out there is where hope lives, I think. Nature trying to rebuild itself after whatever went wrong that destroyed this place.

This morning, I didn't find much of anything happening in the area, which is a good thing. Otherwise, it meant someone was having a very bad day. And while that would break up the monotony, I certainly wouldn't wish for it.

I land gently on top of the tallest thing still standing in this wreck of a city. In my world, this was Oakland's Tribune Tower, an icon of the city appearing on postcards and in movies and television shows shot here. But in this bizarro, post-apocalyptic version of my world, the neon sign hanging on all four sides of the twenty-two-story tower's top never spelled Tribune. The only letters remaining are O and E on one side and L on another. What it used to say has stumped me for all the years I've been here.

I roost like a gargoyle, the sharp claws of my limbs resting on the clock facing southeast. I'm lost in thought for a long time—so long I'm afraid I may actually be turning to stone when somewhere below, the monsters roar. I open my jaws and give an answering bellow, mine even louder, echoing across the splintered husks of buildings, the shattered streets and rusted-out hollows of old cars. This city, this version of my city, is nothing but ghosts now.

Instead of quieting down in response to my call, the bellows and snarls intensify. My ears perk up. They sound like that when they've homed in on prey. Someone down there is having a very bad day, after all. It's been a while, several months at least, since any human has wandered into the city. My heartbeat speeds at the thought—I hate that somebody's in danger, but the chance to talk to another person, to break up the endless isolation and loneliness, excites me. I can hate myself for it later. For now, I need to get over there.

A high-pitched scream tears through the bass of rumbles and growls just as my wings catch air. A woman.

It's coming from the direction of the lake—Lake Merritt in my world, but I don't know what it was called here. So much of what remains in this strange place is the same as home, even down to the remains of Fairyland, the children's amusement park that Sonya loved so much.

I flap my enormous wings, blowing away some of the fog. I don't really need to see to find the creatures I call kaiju; I can feel them. They exist as a low-level hum in my head, another presence sort of like the Intruder—that thing that took up residence inside my brain and makes my body change—except the kaiju feel very different.

The screaming continues as I race to the lake shore. Here, the island of Alameda to the west of the city is virtually nonexistent. There's a thin strip of land where it once was, maybe just its highest elevations, and the waters of the San Francisco Bay reach almost all the way to Lake Merritt, flooding a portion of the city I knew.

Was it climate change? Or a result of whatever destroyed the world and killed most of the people? Did the same thing create the kaiju? Twelve years here and I still have no idea.

I land on the parched earth beyond the lake, and the ground shakes. The roars of monsters and the human screaming stop for a moment, maybe recognizing an even larger threat. The fog is still heavy, clinging to the ground the way it does until early afternoon on most days. It cloaks me, which is for the best. I sense the kaiju, four of them, moving together toward their prey, forcing the woman toward the waters of the lake.

Anger building inside me, I open my jaws and let out a rumbling roar. It vibrates deep within my chest, and I have to pull myself back along with the rising rage. Don't want to lose control. I can barely glimpse the woman through the thick fog, but she's human, and she's in danger.

The kaiju turn to face my threat, temporarily ignoring their hunt.

LEAVE. My command is mental, sent along the pathways of that awareness of them that lives in my mind. The literal curse I bear that makes me able to control them.

The pain starts immediately. Faster than ever before. A few years ago, it would take hours of controlling the creatures before the aching started behind my eyes. Now it's instantaneous. In this form, it barely resonates, but it will be very bad soon.

However, I push past it, ignoring it to focus. *LEAVE THIS WOMAN ALONE.*

The kaiju shudder and start to back away. I move toward the woman, then remember I'm in monster form. She'll be terrified.

Staying shrouded in mist, I focus on the Intruder. Call on the thing that's taken up residence inside of me and lets me change back to my normal form. To a human man. It complies.

I wonder if it always will. Will there come a day when I want to shift back and can't?

The curse is magic, so I still have my clothes on, not like in the werewolf stories I grew up with or that book series the girls at school all loved where boys turned into giant wolves but had to run around buck naked when they shifted back. Small mercies.

The kaiju try to fight the control, but I push harder, though it's even more painful while I'm human and the connection is weaker. My head rings like the inside of a bell, but the scaly creatures with their red eyes keep moving away. Not far enough for my liking, but to a relatively safe distance. They're not particularly speedy, so even if I were to somehow lose control of them, getting away should still be possible.

I approach the woman, who holds some kind of flashlight with a brilliant blue light. She's brown-skinned, dressed head to toe in red, though her outfit is dirty and torn. Her chest is heaving, pupils dilated. She may be in shock.

"Are you all right? Did they hurt you?" I ask, scanning her for injuries. The kaiju's poisonous claws are deadly, but I don't see any visible wounds on her. She stares at me wildly, still gasping for breath.

"My name is Victor. If you come with me, I can take you

someplace safe." I keep my voice low and soft, not wanting to spook her, and hold out a hand, hoping she'll take it. This close, I see the smoothness of her brown skin. Her hair is matted and dirty, pulled back into a dented Afro puff. She looks like she's been through a hard time, even before the kaiju attack.

I'm close to her now, hovering my hand over hers, when she finally shakes herself free of the grip of terror. She blinks. Frowns. Then takes a step back and starts searching the ground.

"I...I can't go, yet. I need my pack."

The monsters are pushing at my mental control. The bell in my head crashes in a consistent rhythm. Nausea rises. My nose stings, and wetness pools in my nostrils.

The nosebleeds started about a year ago. They're getting worse, too. If I don't get out of here soon, I'll pass out, leaving both of us vulnerable. And I can't control the beasts if I'm unconscious.

The woman turns in a circle, shining her light on the ground. "I thought the knot on the strap would hold," she mutters to herself. "Where is it?"

Not a word of thanks or a smidge of gratitude from this one. It doesn't matter, it *shouldn't* matter. I'd save her regardless, but you know, risking your life to help someone should at least get you a thank you. Was she raised by wolves or something?

But it's like I'm not even here. She's entirely focused on the backpack or whatever that she must have dropped, but the kaiju are growing more restless, pushing against my mental barrier.

LEAVE, I send again, weaker now. Blood drips in a stream from my nose. I swipe it away, anger growing.

"Listen, lady, we have to get out of here. Now."

She holds up a hand. Actually holds up a hand to me. "Not yet. It's got to be around here somewhere."

I stare, incredulous. Where in the hell did this chick come from? Well, I know where she's going, because black starts creeping into the edges of my vision. I need to get her the ten blocks back to safety, to the place where the creatures don't go, where I've ensured they *can't* go. So, there's only one thing left for me to do.

She's about five-foot-six, not tiny, but not difficult for me to lift. I stoop down, grab her knees, and pull her into a fireman's carry.

"What in Origin's name are you doing? Let go of me immediately!"

I ignore her yells and the pounding of her fists against my back, grip her tighter, and run.

The monsters roar behind me, and the sound shuts her up, finally. Then I'm racing through the fog with my very ungrateful companion in my arms.

TWO

Celena
——————

I CAN'T TELL whether the Revokers are chasing us or not. They're still growling and snapping their jaws, and the sounds don't seem like they're getting farther away. But bumping along on this man's shoulders—the man who kidnapped me— is making me nauseous.

"Let me down," I say with venom.

"Not a chance, sweetheart," he replies.

"Do you know who I am?"

"You were about to be kaiju food. Where I come from, folks usually at least say thank you to the person who saved their life."

I press my lips shut. Nimali princesses do not say thank you. Whoever he is, he should know that. I didn't glimpse his shifted form through the heavy mist, but he's definitely a predator, loud and intimidating enough to scare the Revokers away. His roar was unlike any I've heard before. Deeper and more gravelly than even my father's, though there's no chance he's a dragon.

"What kind of daimon do you have?" I ask, but he doesn't reply.

He leaps nimbly over an upturned bit of asphalt in the

street, still running swiftly. A muscular arm is wrapped around my thigh as I'm draped over his shoulders. He's strong, that much is clear, and in another context, being pressed so close to him wouldn't be so bad. He even smells nice, something spicy that I can't place.

I would have thought he was one of our patrols, the Air Nimali who periodically monitor the eastern region, but he's dressed strangely in pants that are somewhere between Umber brown and drudge gray. His shirt is green, a color favored by the Fai, as I understand, but I'm certain he shifted forms.

Is he some kind of rogue Nimali living out here on his own, or perhaps he's traveled from some other Nimali clan? Though I'm not aware of any others that survived the Sorrows. Is he an exile who somehow kept his daimon?

"I must be heavy. Let me down." Again, he doesn't spare a breath to answer; however, the low howls of the deadly predators who nearly caught me reply instead.

"Are they following us?" My voice is nothing but a tremor.

"Ding, ding, ding," he says, making a sharp turn. I have no idea why he made that sound. Maybe he speaks another language. But it seems to be an affirmative response to my question.

Killed by Revokers, that would be a fitting end to the disaster that this mission has been. I was so sure, so confident when I left…When was that, even? I lost track of time down there in the tunnels.

It had started well. I'd crossed the bay in the small boat without incident, then began searching for the markers my mother mentioned that would lead into the tunnels. But the landscape must have changed in the past twenty-five years. Landmarks she described were nowhere to be found. I spent days searching before finally realizing that the flooding had progressed, covering the land and the tunnel entrances.

Knowing that being on open land would mean facing the Revokers, I sailed up and down the shore until I finally found a way into the underground passages. But I quickly got lost, and stayed lost for…I don't know how long. It was dark and damp and cold down there. Tiny scurrying creatures and insects and dirt and muck made up my entire world.

The shoulder strap of my pack caught on some old rusted pipes and tore, and it kept falling off. Then, when I finally, finally, found a sign Mother had mentioned in her vids and emerged out in the open, I was met almost immediately with the horrifying creatures I'd been hoping desperately to avoid.

I am grateful to the strange man who saved my life, but in the commotion, my pack slipped off again and with it everything I have left of my mother. The tablet with her vids was in there, its power cell running low but still functional. Her voice was the only thing that kept me sane through the dark days I spent underground.

Beneath me, the man grunts as he pulls open a heavy door. Lost in my thoughts, I get only a glimpse of the outside of the building we enter, and then I'm being dumped unceremoniously on the floor while he bars the door with heavy-looking metal beams.

It's dark in here, the only light coming from high above. A large hole goes straight up through several stories of the building, all the way to the roof, which is no longer intact. It's like something large fell all the way down through this structure, through five or six levels it must be. Light filters down, but cloudy with a greenish cast, like there is some translucent substance up there covering the hole.

Unlike back home, where the buildings in use by our clan have been reconstructed by engineers, this place, while upright, still bears the marks of the Sorrows. I sit up on the filthy floor, tiled in an alternating green and white pattern, and get my bearings. The wall of doors leading outside is barricaded, looking to be welded shut with thick sheets of metal. The only exit I see is the single door the man just barred.

He leans heavily against it, breathing deeply.

"I told you I was heavy."

"It's not you, sweetheart." When he looks up, blood dots his upper lip.

Alarm shoots through me, and I scrabble up to my feet. "Are you ill?"

He takes a step forward and then collapses in a heap. Part of me wants to rush forward to see if I can help, but the other part needs to get back out there, find my pack, and stay on the mission. I've already been gone for so long and wasted so much time.

However, the thundering roars of the Revokers are closer now. They *were* following. Can they get in? This place must be safe—the work on the doors looks to have taken some time and no little amount of effort. I'm not entirely sure I have the strength to lift the massive beam from the door anyway, and even if I could, the Revokers are too close.

Still, I'm torn. This man did help me, but that doesn't mean he's not dangerous. The mystery of who he is and what he's doing here persists. Yet at the moment, without my pack and all my supplies, he is my best bet. I kneel next to him and check his pulse. Strong. At least he isn't dead.

The only thing I have on me is the canteen belted to my waist, so I spare a few drops of water and use my sleeve to wipe away his blood. I'm filthy anyway, so what's a little more grime?

His face is all angles and lines. Lean and somewhat sharp with golden toasted freckled skin and kinky dark reddish hair, cut short. Old scars, from claws of some kind, run down the side of his face into his hairline. They're silvery white in the gloom, pale streaks bisecting an otherwise beautifully masculine face.

His eyes flutter, and he comes to quickly, sitting up so fast that I have to shift away to avoid us bumping noses. Dark bronze eyes lock onto me and a light of recognition flares. "Do I…Do I know you?" he asks.

"All Nimali do. I am Celena."

"Victor." He looks down at me and then up. "Nimali? The beast men, right?"

I shake my head in disbelief. "How hard did you hit your head? I take it you're not from Aurum."

His forehead bunches. "The city across the bay? No. That's where you're from?"

"Yes. I am Celena Radasdaughter, princess of the Nimali."

His eyes show no recognition, but a brow rises. "Princess?" His lips quirk as though he finds this funny. "I guess we haven't met then."

My shoulders stiffen. "You are a shifter. What type of daimon do you have?"

"Daimon?" He looks legitimately confused, which takes me aback.

"I didn't get a good look at your daimon's form, but it was large. Are you a Land, Air, or Fire? You didn't come out of the lake, that's for certain."

"I have no idea what you're talking about," he says.

"You don't know what kind of shifter you are?" I ask incredulously.

His head drops, shoulders, too. Then he moves to his feet with effort. I stand as well. Overall, he appears to have recovered from whatever happened to him.

"I do…turn into something." The roars outside get louder, making me shiver. "Don't worry. They'll stay out there for a while and then move on. We're safe in here. They can't get in."

I look around again. The walls are likely thick, and I'm assuming he's sealed up any gaps. Revokers can't fly, so they can't get to the upper-story windows. Still, this building seems like flimsy protection.

"How can you be certain?"

He gives me a wry look. "I've been here for years."

That gives me a little relief. "When they go away, I need to get back out there. I dropped something very important—"

"Do you know what a parallel is?" He rudely interrupts me.

I take a deep breath for patience. "It seems you need to learn some manners, Victor. And of course, I know what a parallel is."

"Manners says the woman who still hasn't thanked me for saving her ass."

My nostrils flare and eyes narrow. Never mind that he's right. I suppose the rules I'm used to don't apply in this place. "Thank you," I say through gritted teeth.

"Was that so hard?" His grin is pure insouciance and laced with a disturbing amount of charm. "So, do you have a parallel?"

This line of questioning is disturbing, rubbing against the raw places inside of me that scream of failure. "No, I do not."

He peers at me closely, scanning up and down my body like he's trying to see something deep within me. This perusal is beyond inappropriate—so rude and disrespectful that I should slap him. But then his head tilts and I get a little lost.

At home, no one is allowed to just gape at me like this. Unless they're a Cardinal, most people don't even meet my eyes. They bow and act deferentially. All the while treating me like something breakable and delicate. They do not stare.

But his eyes on me are almost like a touch. Being touched is also something verboten for the princess of the clan. Yet Victor hauled me against him like it was nothing.

I force myself to take a step back. "What?"

The expression of concentration clears. "When I woke up, I thought..." He breathes deeply, seeming to shake himself internally. "Doesn't matter. You can't go back out there."

"The Revokers seem to be afraid of your daimon. Perhaps you could come with me and—"

"Revokers?" He tilts his head again in question.

I blink. "Red-eyed, winged monsters trying to kill me? You are familiar with them, are you not?"

He snorts. "I've been calling them kaiju in my head all these years."

"Kaiju? I've never heard that term before. Where are you from?" The question has been gnawing at me. Plus, how did he come to live in this isolated place?

"You wouldn't believe me if I told you," he says with a sad smile.

Before the Sorrows, there were many clans in many places, but we have not been in communication with any others for decades. "Are you from another clan? Are there others here?" But instead of answering, he begins to walk away.

"Don't walk away when I'm talking to you, Victor."

He just laughs. "You may be a princess over there, but here, you're not the boss of me." Then he leaves me alone in the lobby. The angry cries of the Revokers start up again, startling me, so I follow him down a darkened hallway.

"Is there anyone else here that I can talk to?"

"Just me, sweetheart."

I swallow. "You live here all alone?"

He says nothing.

"For how long?"

"Since I got here. Twelve years ago."

The hallway ends in a door, which he holds open for me. I pass, looking directly into his eyes, but they've been blanked of all emotion. "I suppose that explains your lack of manners."

His mask cracks into a smile, and he starts walking again. "Not a fan of me lack of airs and graces," he says in a strange accent. He's a very odd man, but that thought quickly flees as I get a glimpse of the surroundings.

The space is wide; perhaps it was once another lobby.

There are doorways leading out to other places, but the center of the room is clear. On the floor, a dazzling mural has been painted. It's a city scene, but a very different version of the city. This one is alive and full of people and vehicles.

Instead of cracked pavement mostly overtaken by tough greenery, the streets are solid and intact. Every building is whole and complete with real glass glinting in the windows.

Smiles and laughs light all the faces with joy. Children play with balls and chase one another. Adults sit at tables in an outdoor café. In a lush, green park, musicians play instruments and sing on a stage. This is a portrait of a lively, happy, thriving place. Even the reclaimed Nimali sections of Aurum cannot hope to compare.

I goggle, eyes wide. Something inside me knows that Victor painted this. He has imagined in great detail what life must have been like before the Sorrows. I look up at him, unable to speak.

He's staring off into the distance and stuffs his hands into the pockets of his trousers, totally ignorant of the pure awe I'm experiencing. "Sometimes people pass through here on their way someplace else," he says. "East, usually. There's rumors of a city out that way. Someplace safe that's rebuilding. I help travelers get through from time to time."

I swallow and try to corral my features into something slightly less indecorous. "You have never wanted to go with them?"

He glances at me. "You're definitely better dressed and better fed than anyone I've seen before, even with all the dirt."

There is no need to reference my filthy state. "Princess," I say, pointing to myself.

He laughs. This time, full out. The sound is raspy and hoarse, as if unused to being released into the world, and it's captivating.

I clench my jaw, tearing my gaze away from his mouth and lips and this small glimpse of mirth. "When they leave"—

I point back toward the lobby and the beasts outside—"will you help me get my pack? Wait, you've been here twelve years? Do you know where the bliss pool is?"

"Bliss pool?" His brows rise.

How is it that he doesn't know anything? He's no better than a child. "Bliss. The spirit energy in liquid form that we use to travel to the Origin and leash our daimons. Do you call it something else?"

His expression goes from confused to carefully blank. For the first time, I sense he actually does know what I'm talking about. "Why would you want to go there?"

"To leash a daimon, of course!"

He recoils as if he finds the idea abhorrent. "Come on, princess. You want to get cleaned up, I'm guessing."

So many questions vie for prominence in my mind. Maybe he is an exile from somewhere and blames his daimon? Or… Well, I just don't know anything about him or why he's here, and he's not exactly forthcoming, though the answers are likely important.

He leads me to a set of steps heading down. They've been patched but seem to be in good repair. At the bottom, he stops to light a lantern with a strange metal contraption. It sparks with actual fire, which he uses to light the wick. If I wasn't so sure he'd shifted forms, I'd think he was Fai. Then again, without bliss, he couldn't power any advanced technology, so he'd need to live like some kind of barbarian.

I hear water, and we emerge in a muggy, dark room that has a pit dug out in the center filled with liquid. Judging by the temperature in here, the water is warm.

"Used to be a swimming pool, but I rigged it up so it connects to a natural hot spring." He shrugs, then scratches his head. "There's a um, sleeping bag over there." He waves vaguely into the opposite corner. "Bathroom through those doors."

It's not a huge space and there are no windows, so it feels

safe. Just as I'm scanning the area, he sets down the lantern and leaves, slamming the door behind him.

"Victor?"

I go to the door and try to open it, but it's locked.

"Sorry, princess. I know you're itching to leave, but you can't just yet." His voice is slightly muffled through the thick door.

I try the handle again, pulling on it with all my might. "You're locking me in here? You're keeping me prisoner?"

"Not forever." There seems to be regret in his voice. "But you just might be the key to breaking my curse."

"What curse?"

"You asked what kind of shifter I am. Well, I'm one of them. One of those Revokers, you called them? In fact, I'm their king."

THREE

Victor

SHE's quiet for a long time after I make my announcement. I hold my breath, pressing my ear against the heavy door, waiting for her to say something, anything. Locking her in the pool was a dick move, but desperate times and all. I'm about to turn away, figuring that her disgust with me has silenced her when she finally speaks.

"You can't be a Revoker, that is impossible." Her voice is low and sort of cajoling, like she's trying to reason with a crazy person. "Revokers have no human form. They don't… They don't shift as we do."

I shrug, though she can't see me. "Yeah, I think I'm the only one who can change shapes. And I can fly, while their wings seem mostly decorative. They don't seem to have any humanity in them at all, but I can control them…to an extent. You saw that."

She pauses like she's weighing her words. "You don't seem to know or understand very much about what happens here. Wherever you're from is different?"

"Very."

"So why have you locked me in here? You said something about a curse?"

I lean back against the door, exhausting pulling at me. "My curse is to become one of them. Like some sort of demented werewolf, only I turn into a scaly monster. The old wizard dude said that the only way out was to find my parallel. I didn't even know what that meant, but he told me it was a person, and I would know them when I met them. I think…" It sounds stupid to say out loud, but I press on. "I think it may be you. I recognized something in you."

"Old wizard dude?"

My head is pounding, and I need to eat something after passing out. I push away from the wall. "Can't really go into it all right now. I just need some time to figure things out."

Her voice rises. "I'm certain you can 'figure things out' without imprisoning me in this dark bathing chamber!"

I admit I haven't thought this all the way through, or really at all. And I don't expect her to understand, but I answer her anyway. "Listen, you're the one who wanted to go back out there with the monsters. I'm just keeping you safe from yourself and them while I get a chance to see if you can break the curse. A lot more than just my life depends on it."

"Like what?" She sounds pouty through the door.

"Like all of humanity."

Her voice turns softer again, trying to trap this fly with some honey. "I admit that I don't understand what has happened to you, but there's no way to tell if I'm your parallel without me leashing a daimon. They're the spirits that lives inside us that allow us to shift forms."

The Intruder, I think. They call it a daimon.

"I don't have one," she continues. "That's why I came all the way out here. So if you just let me out, I can find the bliss pool and do my trial and then I'll have a daimon and we can know for certain if we're parallels."

Can I believe her? She wants to get out and leave, that much is clear, as would anybody. Plus, it's obvious this one is used to getting exactly what she wants. The old wizard didn't say anything about daimons or spirits, but it sort of makes sense. The Intruder inside me feels like a consciousness. I get emotions off it, even if it can't speak to me directly.

I rub at my chest, trying to ease the pain within. It's pounding in time with my heart.

Visions of those early days, when I was still coming to grips with what had happened, sweep over me. With being here in this strange world, torn away from everything and everyone I knew. Dropped in a wasteland with no idea how to survive. I'd had to learn.

A few weeks after I got here and all that shit went down with the wizard, I met other people for the first time. Nine of them in total, two families traveling together, heading east, following rumors of settlements that way. I came across them over in Piedmont, squatting in a big house on a hill that had survived the apocalypse pretty much intact.

The smell of smoke had drawn me there, excited out of my mind to have someone to talk to. They were surprised to see me and, after the initial suspicion, welcomed me warmly. I was just a skinny sixteen-year-old kid.

They shared their food and told me about their lives, trying to make light of some pretty terrible situations. That night, I'd slept on the porch of the house thinking that maybe I could go with them. Find some kind of community here, even if I'd never get to go back home.

But then the kaiju came.

They must have been drawn to the noise or the smoke or something. I had a warning, being able to sense them once they got into proximity. I'd figured out what that strange knowing inside of me meant and woke everyone up, alerting them to the danger.

They were packed and ready to go when six of the creatures approached, their red eyes shining in the darkness. That same knowing told me they wanted to kill me most of all. But they'd be happy enough with the others. So I figured I'd draw them away.

It almost worked, but two of the creatures didn't follow. I was still learning how to control them and wasn't good at it.

That family. Their screams echoed in my skull nonstop for months. Years. I had the power to save them, but not the skill. I could have done so much more. When they died, suddenly there were nine more monsters. The kaiju repopulate themselves like zombies from dead bodies. And I realized my failure was so much worse than I thought.

After that, I started taking shit seriously. I practiced every day, seeking out the monsters until they surrounded me and then forcing my control over them. Eventually figured out if I shifted in to their form, something I hated at the time—still hate, if I'm honest—they listened better. But the guilt, even now it nearly forces me to my knees.

I've lost a few others over the years, but only when I didn't get there fast enough. So I started patrolling. Forcing myself to shift so I could fly and keep an eye out. All the while knowing that if I found my parallel—*when* I found them, because it's the only hope I've had—then together we could destroy the kaiju once and for all and I'd be free.

"I'm sorry, princess. I can't be sure you're telling the truth. You'd say anything to get out of there. I just need some time to see if anything changes. To see if the curse breaks."

Honestly, I don't even know what the end of this nightmare will look like. Will all the kaiju just drop dead? Will it take time? Will the Intruder, the daimon inside me, flee forever? Will I be able to return home?

Something thumps like maybe she's stomping her foot. "You will release me this instant. You are lucky we're so far away; I could have the entirety of the Nimali forces rain down destruction on you for this…this impertinence!"

That actually pulls a chuckle out of me. "Where are they,

huh? Why are you here all alone? Why didn't your folks send an honor guard or something with you?"

Silence.

I don't know her story, and I am sorry for doing this to her, but I can't let the chance pass me by. I stumble away, gripping my pounding head.

"I'll be back. Don't worry, this is temporary just until I figure things out."

The sound of a princess screaming obscenities I've never even heard before follows me as I go.

FOUR

Celena

ASIDE FROM THE safe rooms that I'm shuttled to whenever the emergency alarm goes off, I've never been in a prison before. I distinctly dislike it. The walls are drab and ugly, covered in the same smooth tiles that are on the floor. They are cracked in a great many places and patched over. It's warm but too muggy and there's no way I'm touching that disgusting pile of fabric Victor called a "sleeping bag." It looks dingy and stained.

Who in Origin's name does he think he is locking me away because of some curse? Curses aren't real. But of course, someone who's never heard of bliss and doesn't know what Revokers are called wouldn't know that. What sort of backwater hick clan did he come from, anyway? This whole situation is preposterous, and I need to get out of here immediately.

I crouch on my haunches near the door. If I had a daimon, just about any kind of daimon really, I could escape so easily. I'd have strength and maybe claws or powerful paws to break down the door. Even a Water daimon could swim down into the hot springs he described and find a way to the ocean. But I'm just a weak human with no spirit within to lend me their abilities.

I shoot to my feet and bang on the door for so long, my hands begin to ache and feel bruised. He's ignoring me. Or he's elsewhere in the building and can't hear me. Emotions shift like lightning, fear to anger to regret to guilt to rage. Finally, clutching my throbbing hands to my chest, I start to think.

There must be a way out of here. This Victor character is not some kidnapping mastermind, so this place can't possibly be that secure. I search every inch of the room, and the adjoining rooms: two old bathing facilities and one closet full of defunct machinery and dust. The place is actually cleaner than I originally thought, and if there are weak spots in the walls, ceiling, or floor, I don't have the strength or the tools to manipulate them.

Defeat claws at me. Yet another failure. Can I do anything right? I was so certain, so confident, and now look at me...

Time passes. Hours most likely as I huddle on the hard tiles of the floor, awash in shame. The warmth of the bathing waters calls to me, but I don't want to be naked and vulnerable in them. The sound of footsteps has me scurrying over toward the door.

A spicy, aromatic scent filters in. He must be bringing me food. My stomach growls and then clenches painfully. I can't remember my last meal. At some point when I was stuck underground, I started halving my rations to make them last longer, so it's been weeks since I've had a truly satisfying meal.

The door snicks open and I stand to face him, then freeze. I have no plan. I can't take him physically. While he's not huge and bulky, he's taller than me, and I've already felt the power in those lean muscles. Plus, he has a beast of some kind inside him that he can call on at any time. Not a Revoker though, because that's impossible.

"Hungry?" His voice is gravelly.

"If I say no, will you starve me to death?"

He snorts. "*You'd* be starving yourself to death, princess."

He carries a rough plank of wood, using it as a tray. On it sits a metal canister and a plate of unfamiliar food in strange shapes.

"What is this?"

"I call it chicken curry. Tastes nothing like it, but it's the best I can do with no chicken and no spices." He laughs to himself.

Yet again, I have no idea what he's talking about, but whatever herbs he has available, the food certainly smells good. I would only hurt myself by not eating it; however, I still look at him with suspicion.

"You haven't drugged this, have you?"

"With what? Can't exactly walk down to the Rite Aid to grab some roofies."

The nonsense words he says make me shake my head.

"Besides, if I'd wanted to kill you, wouldn't I have let the monsters do it? What did you call them, Revocaters?"

"Revokers."

"Yeah, them."

"How are you one of them? How are you their king, if you don't even know what they are?"

He shrugs. "Hasn't come up before. They're not exactly chatty."

"But you can control them?"

"To a degree. Enough to stop them from murdering someone close by."

He sets the tray down on the ground, then backs up as if he's afraid I'd claw him. Could I? Even to save my life? Though at the moment, my life does not appear to be in danger.

"Maybe we can help each other," I say diplomatically.

He raises a brow, but doesn't move to leave.

"I need to do my daimon trial in a pure bliss pool. There's one around here, there must be. You say you got here twelve years ago?" He nods. "You must have been a teenager then. So you leashed your daimon here?"

He looks uncomfortable and purses his lips, making me think I'm right.

"I'm probably looking for the same place where you got your daimon." Perhaps that's why he's so powerful. Maybe he leashed something so strong, it gave him additional powers over the Revokers. This could be exactly what I need to save my city and my people.

My eyes grow large, and I rush toward him. He steps back, alarmed and wary. "What if I could also leash a daimon that can control the Revokers? If the bliss pool is responsible, we could destroy them together. Parallel or no."

His face is a rictus of misery. "I want you to break my curse, not take it on yourself." Then he just peers into my eyes for a long moment, searching for something.

"It was there before, but now I don't see it." He shakes his head, leaving me confused. Is he angry? His moods seem to change like the wind.

I try another tack. "My father will pay any price for me. If it's supplies you want, he'll give anything to have me back safe."

The corner of Victor's lip curls. "He doesn't have what I want."

"He's the king of the Nimali! He's a dragon! If he doesn't have what you want, he can get it. Just let me out of here. I'm going to go crazy trapped in this dark, muggy room. How could keeping me here possibly help with your curse?"

He holds his head in his hands like my tantrum has hurt him. With him breathing heavily and standing there like that, I feel a little sorry for Victor. Something is going on with his mind, and if he's having mental health challenges, then he'll need to be put down.

A pang hits me. That's what Father always does, but it's never quite sat right with me. The brutality of it always chafed. There must be a better way to handle such illnesses of the mind, though I admit I don't know what they are. However, Father always says that wasting food on those who are ill-suited to contribute to our way of life weakens the clan.

I don't want to be weak, but that has never felt like strength.

How can I get this man to do what I want, though? Whether I try to be sweet or commanding, he doesn't respond to either. What is left in my arsenal?

"I can feel your brain working, princess," he says from behind his hands. It looks like he's gotten himself together. He straightens, dropping his arms. "I know you've had everything handed to you on a silver platter your entire life." He looks significantly at the tray he brought my food in on, still on the ground. "But I'm not your servant or your subject. And I'm sorry about locking you in here. Normally, doing something that is sure to get you killed would be your choice, but if you *are* the one who can break this curse, then together we can end the Revokers. Forever. I can't let anything, even you, jeopardize that."

His demeanor has shifted. He's not demanding or throwing a tantrum, he's being genuine. Speaking to me like I'm a person, not a princess. The way virtually no one else but Dominga ever does.

Maybe that's the way I should treat him as well.

I take a deep breath, dropping all semblance of pretense. "I don't understand this curse you believe you have. But if there's a way for me to break it, I will help you. I swear it. But can you help me, too? If I promise not to run out recklessly into the arms of the Revokers?"

His jaw tenses. "Help you get to the…the bliss pool? So, you can transform into one of those creatures?" A brow raises.

"Not one of those creatures. People don't shift into Revokers. But I want to be a dragon. Though a lion would do. Perhaps a gorilla. Something strong, but preferably a predator that would allow me to step up and become the queen my people need. A daimon that would allow me to protect my clan."

My mother's words have never left me. Her faith in me is strong even from her place now in the Origin. My father's expectations and demands are weighty as well. I came here for this, and I'm not going back without it.

Victor's gaze is full of sympathy. While that chafes—I don't want pity from anyone—I think I'm getting through to him. He scans the room behind me and grimaces. "That place, the bliss pool, is nothing but misery. I don't know why you'd want to go there. But I guess you can stay someplace else here, while I figure things out."

I nod, happy at least with that small gesture. "Anywhere is better than here."

He scrutinizes me for another moment. "All right then. Follow me."

FIVE

Celena

I CARRY the tray while he holds the lantern, and we head back up the stairs. And then up yet another staircase. It's obvious that a lot of work has been done over a long period of time to make this place into something resembling a home. There is evidence of repairs everywhere, a patchwork quality to the walls and floors that is very rough in places, but grows more refined. Likely showing the passage of the years. Twelve years. All of them spent here?

The path we take is free of dust and debris, though I can tell there are large portions of the building not in use where the cleaning is not as meticulous. However, the spaces that he uses have all been decorated with intricately painted murals. They depict a variety of locations and scenes, from forests to meadows to the stars in the sky and other planets. Victor walks quickly, his legs longer than mine, so I don't get the chance to study the art, but I hope to at some point. They're truly remarkable.

I open my lips to praise his painting, then think better of it. He's still my captor. He does not deserve my compliments, and I don't think they'd soften him to my plight at all. We walk down another hall with yet another mural, this one of a sunset over a sandy beach, and then he leads me to the end of the corridor and a closed door. He opens it with a flourish, ushering me inside. I'm completely unprepared for what I find before me.

"It's a library. An old-fashioned one," I say, craning my neck to take in the rows and rows of shelving reaching high over my head. All of them filled with paper books. I've never seen so much paper before. Could all these books be in readable condition? My chest expands with awe.

Multiple stories of shelving rise above me with light streaming down from the clear ceiling. "What is the roof made of? How does rain and the elements not ruin all of this…this paper?"

He looks at me askance. "It's glass."

I squint up. "Glass? Windows? How? All glass shattered during the Sorrows."

"Basically just fire and sand," he replies with a shrug. "There's books on how to make glass in here. Books on everything. I've learned a lot."

I walk further into the room and turn in a slow circle. Hundreds, thousands of books surround us. "You've read them all?"

He stuffs his free hand into the pocket of his strange trousers again. "Yup."

I forcibly close my mouth. The wonder of this sight is tempered somewhat by the loneliness he must have experienced here for so long.

"Is this more to your liking, princess?" he asks wryly.

"Yes. Yes, this is very much to my liking. I spent time in our library at home, but there were no books."

"What did you have in the library, then?"

His confusion is almost comical. "Data streams. Paper is far too delicate. How did these books survive?"

"Place was a wreck when I got here. Took a long time to get it all organized and there were a ton of books that were water damaged and had to be used for kindling, basically. But I don't know, this building is old with sturdy walls. The ceiling was intact when I got here, the hole came...later."

Sounds like there's a story there, but I don't get a chance to ask before he's moving forward across an open space littered with long tables and chairs. Books are stacked on them in piles. I get a glimpse of their spines. There are volumes on science, engineering, gardening, history, economics, sports, sociology.

We head for an alcove set up between two of the columns, which hold up the second level. "There's a bed here. I'll change the sheets."

"Is this where you sleep?" I ask, looking at the mattress on the floor, less than half the size of my bed at home. The shelves next to it here bear his personal items: a pile of neatly folded clothing; a book he must be reading, place marked with a scrap of fabric; a small box of salvaged odds and ends that I have no names for.

"There's no shortage of space. I sleep a lot of places." He gets busy stripping the sheets off the bed and goes to another open shelf where more linens are waiting crisply folded.

It's just as well he's doing it; I've never made a bed before. However, instead of watching how the task is done, I turn back to the rest of the large room. Fire-burning lanterns sit atop all the tables, the surfaces of which, as well as the floor and pillars, bear evidence of Victor's artistic handiwork. Instead of murals, these are painted with smaller images. Tiny animals and plants, scrollwork and decorative touches. All heartbreakingly beautiful.

Victor finishes with the bed and then backs away. "Bathroom is through there." He points to the opposite corner. "No shower or anything, though the water's hot. Let me know if you ever want to take that bath." He looks at my still-filthy form significantly. "And eat. I'll, ah, I'll be back to check on you soon."

I spin around as he heads to the door, long legs eating up the space faster than I can follow. "Wait!"

But he's already gone. And the sound of the door locking makes me let out a scream. This library is amazing and much better than that stuffy room. But I'm still a prisoner.

I need to get out of here. I must find the bliss pool—with or without his aid—do my trials, and leash a daimon. A dragon. Then go back home triumphant and worthy of my birthright. Become the queen who is needed. There are no other options.

So, I search the walls and corners. Climb the ladders to the upper levels and spend the next few hours trying to find any way out of here.

The ceiling—the glass—is a weak point. But without wings of my own, I can't get all the way up there. None of the ladders will go so high, and climbing the bookshelves will likely result in me breaking a bone. Without a Fai to heal me, I'd be done for.

Frustrated, I fall into a chair at one of the long tables. The light overhead is slowly dying with the aging of the afternoon. The lovely smelling food has cooled, but I eat it anyway, needing to regain my strength. The textures are unusual, but the flavors are pleasant. I have no idea what I'm eating, but I clear the plate, anyway.

All the while, knowing I will have to bide my time and determine a way out of this.

Failure is not an option.

SIX

Celena

I MUST HAVE FALLEN asleep at the table. When I open my eyes, sunlight streams in through the glass overhead. Now that I can see it more clearly in the bright light, it's made up of a patchwork of small squares with some thicker and cloudier than others. Evidently, Victor grew better at glassmaking along the way.

An aromatic scent hits my nose and I look down. Victor has been here. The tray sits on the table across from me, holding a covered plate. My stomach growls and I drag it to myself. It's still warm.

The food is as odd-looking as ever, but the smell is delightful. Green leaves that look freshly plucked out of the dirt give me pause. Nimali food is highly processed, so that the optimal nutrients are included. Of course, he would have no way to do that here without the bliss and the engineers and scientists.

I gingerly pluck a vibrant leaf from the plate and place it in my mouth. It's surprisingly crunchy. As my jaw works, the flavor hits my tongue. Is this really what raw produce tastes like, or did he enhance it in some way? This primitive fare might actually be growing on me.

Before I know it, I've cleaned the plate. The weeks underground in the darkness, cold and afraid and on half-rations, took their toll. I'm always ravenously hungry now. As I shift in my chair, my own body odor hits me, making my eyes water. I probably should have taken that bath.

I investigate the bathroom he pointed out to me, pleased to find running hot water in the sink as well as a stack of towels. It's certainly not my luxurious shower at home, but I'm able to scrub the dirt off my body. Instead of changing back into my muck-encrusted clothing, I don a pair of oversized trousers and a long-sleeved shirt I found on the shelves. They're as soft as moss, a bit threadbare in some places, and though I swim in them, the fabric is comfortable. There's a unique scent to the clothes as well. I bring the collar of the shirt—a faded purple thing—to my nose and inhale. It's heady, warm, and minty, with a hint of sweetness. Is this what Victor smells like?

I drop it quickly, somewhat mortified. The man who trapped me here should not have the nerve to smell so appealing. Squaring my shoulders, I determine to clear my head and focus on my true purpose.

Being locked in a library isn't the worst thing in the world. Until I can get out of here, maybe there is something in these old books that can help me leash a daimon or aid my people once I return. Since the natural light streaming in from overhead is bright, I might as well start reading.

The shelves are organized by subject matter: History, Art, Philosophy, Memoir, Science, Music. Then the many subgenres of fiction. All from before the Sorrows. I realize it must be all human as well, so there will be nothing about daimons, but that doesn't mean they're useless. I run my hands along the spines, just getting a feel for them. All of this knowledge locked away in here. I still don't understand how they all survived the Sorrows?

From what I know, the shaking of the earth, and the storms, and then the responses of the various human governments caused the destruction of most of the world. Calamities and wars brought on more death and devastation. Tempests raged, bombs fell, disease spread. The sky eventually grew poisonous, the very rain tainted.

Daimons helped the Nimali, and I suppose the Fai as well, get through it all. The humans were not so lucky. They were almost completely wiped out. There are survivors living in Aurum in hovels and underground encampments, but they don't affect our lives very much. However, once upon a time, they created amazing archives like this with all of their knowledge.

Recording it all on paper feels like a mistake, though. It's such a delicate material. Incredibly inefficient for storing precious knowledge. The very few books I've seen back home are kept in the vault, and I was admonished as a small girl not to touch them for fear they would crumble under my fingertips.

So it's with great care that I select a volume at random from a low shelf and begin to read.

When I next become aware of my surroundings, Victor stands across from me with a tray in his hands.

"Is it lunchtime?" I exclaim, rising. My body is sore. I haven't moved in what seems like hours. Judging by the sun's position, it *has* been hours.

He smiles. "This place will do that to you." The smile is sad, though.

"You've really read all of them?"

"Many of them twice. Lots of time on my hands."

I can't think of a response, so I don't try. "What's your favorite?" I sit as he slides the tray over to me.

"I like the classics. Frankenstein. Dracula."

I shake my head. "I'm not familiar with human books."

"No, they don't have them here anyway. But there are similar ones. For instance. *Gernsheim* is a story of a female scientist in the 1800s whose husband dies, and she wants to bring him back so badly that she digs him up and reanimates him."

"She brings him back from the dead?" I gape.

"Yeah, but he's different. His personality has shifted and for a long time, she doesn't know why. She tries different experiments on him to try to get him back to his old self, but…" He stops short, and I find I'm hanging on the words. He grins. "I don't want to spoil it. You should read it yourself."

He jumps up and strides to a nearby shelf, then pulls a volume down unerringly. His story sounds even more interesting than the book I was reading about the various wars of the Dytikan Empire, which was fascinating.

Victor plunks the book down before me and then stares at it. "I'm not keeping you here forever, I just…I just need some time to work out what to do. How to know for sure whether you're…"

"Whether I'm your parallel? I'm not lying when I tell you that there's no way to know until I get a daimon."

He frowns, then raps the table with his knuckles and spins around on his heel to leave. Shaking my head, I watch his back.

Once again, I wolf down my meal like a starving animal and then turn to the book he left. The title and author's name are printed in gold on the cover. It's a little faded, but when new it must have been quite lovely.

I flip through the pages, noticing handwritten notes in the margins. The paper itself is brown at the edges, with evidence of moisture darkening the corners. In contrast, the ink of the handwriting is relatively fresh. Did Victor make these notes?

They are nonsensical to me. Why write "This phrase is in the original" with an arrow to an underlined sentence, or "Sounds just like Mary Shelley"? I can't make heads or tails of it, but perhaps it gives me a little insight into his mind. Apparently, it's a chaotic place.

In this land where he's from, do they just eat vegetables from right out of the ground and don't have bliss or daimons? But they do shift forms. How is that possible without a daimon? It's all completely mad. And beyond my ability to determine on my own. In order to escape those spiraling thoughts, I read.

The book is not very long and quite entertaining. It's clear why Victor likes it. I'd never considered whether the story of a woman reanimating her dead husband could hold my interest, but I'm learning all kinds of new things.

Once I'm done, I wander over to the shelf he plucked it from to replace it, and perhaps find another. My finger traces the spines, reading the titles. *Chronicles of the Lost Kingdoms. The Cursed Codex. A Wicked Symphony.* I try to imagine the stories hinted at by the names. However, a thinner volume with a blank spine stands out amid the rest. I slide it off the shelf, fingers enjoying the feel of the soft black leather exterior. Flipping it open, I'm surprised to discover the entire thing is hand-written. And the writing matches the notes in the margins of the book I just read. It's a journal.

I open up to a random page in the middle.

DAY 2,111.

I accepted that I would never see home again a long time ago. Now I wonder if I should survive. Can I take a hunger strike against myself? Against this place I've been taken? Of course then I'll never know why. And seems like I'm the only one holding back the monsters from the gate. If something happens to me, who will protect the people?

———

I GLANCE at the door Victor uses. The sun has grown murky behind cloud cover. I didn't bring my comm, not wanting to be tracked, and I'm out of comm range anyway, so without a daimon's internal sense, I have no idea what the time is. He could be back at any moment, and I don't know if he'd want me reading this, but the urgent need propels me. This is his story. I'm almost certain of it. And I need to start at the beginning. I want to know everything about him. It may be my key to getting out of here.

Day 30.

Found this journal in the Trib Tower. At least that's what it looks like here, though inside there must have been a library instead of a newspaper office and whatever other shit was in there.

I've only stayed here a couple of times, but it looks like the old wizard dude was right. It's the safest place for me to be. He fortified it to be hella strong, so there's that.

This whole thing—it's just too weird. I know I'm crazy. I'm probably in a mental hospital right now, and this is just a dream. Or I'm in a coma and Ma is looking down at my body hooked up to tubes and shit and crying. I didn't want her to have any more pain.

But if I'm writing this down, I should start at the beginning.

Me and El were shooting hoops over at Tech when it happened; the sound of tires screeching was the only warning. I remember that and the look of fear on El's face, and then the gunshots.

I dropped to the ground, but I'd already been hit. El was into some shady shit, and Ma didn't like me hanging with him, but I never thought it would blow back on me. Stupid.

Then I remember the ambulance. The hospital. Nurses. Doctors. Machines. Lots of pain. I went to surgery, and I actually heard the flatline the moment my heart stopped.

Suddenly, I was falling. Dropping through the sky like a missile, scared shitless, wondering if I was descending straight into hell. I was only wearing that thin ass hospital gown, so I was damn near naked. Hit the ground without somehow breaking every bone in my body, which sort of made sense since I figured I was dead anyway.

Then the monsters came.

Red-eyed baby kaiju with claws roaring and snapping their teeth at me.

Now, I wasn't the best person in life—definitely no Mother Teresa—but I wasn't the worst. I listened to my mother as much as any sixteen-year-old did. Took care of my baby sister as much as I could while she was alive. Went to class more than I skipped. Didn't shoplift and never sold drugs or got up to the shit El was into. But I was paying for something. Probably shoulda took my ass to church.

The monsters slashed at me, catching me across the face and chest and legs. I'd thought getting shot hurt, but fuck. I lost consciousness, figuring maybe I was just going to die over and over again as punishment for whatever I'd done. When I came to, this white-haired dude with a bushy gray beard was dragging me down the street by my arms. He looked sort of like a Mexican Gandalf or Dumbledore, only in the face he wasn't actually that old, and he was in bad shape. Bleeding from his nose and ears.

I started struggling to get him to let me go, and he looked down at me. "Good, you're awake," he said. Then started giving me all these instructions, while still dragging me. Even though he looked like he was going to keel over any second, he had that old man strength, and I couldn't get free.

He was ranting about me finding my parallel and being able to defeat the Lost Ones. About staying in the tower, how it was the safest place. Sounded like a bunch of rambling nonsense, and I was pretty disoriented. He stopped suddenly, and I remember the last words clearly. "I don't have much time left, but you have to find her soon. She will make it all worthwhile."

Then he finally let go of my arms, only to nudge me with his foot down into a hole in the ground. I screamed all the way down, tumbling ass first into this warm, oily goo. And then I was someplace else.

Diary, let me tell you, that shit was freaky. It was like I was on the set of a music video. One of those brightly lit, all-white spaces with nothing else around. And there was this voice.

Not a man or woman, just a disembodied voice, like the voice of God or something. It took a second before I could stop freaking out enough to hear what it was saying, but it was talking to me.

It apologized to me. Said it had searched the worlds to find the right one, and I was the only one who fit. That I needed to find my parallel. It was saying the same stuff as the wizard dude, but I was still having a hard time taking it all in.

Then it was over. I woke up floating on my back in that pit of blue goo, but could see the sky overhead. I scrambled out of the liquid, seriously scared when it wasn't wet at all. Managed to climb out of the pit only to find the wizard dead in a heap, bleeding from everywhere—eyes, mouth, chest— and those same red-eyed fucking monsters hovering. I was

---

THE ENTRY ENDS THEN ABRUPTLY. I turn the page to find a new one.

DAY 33.

I don't know why I got so creeped out writing the story down. It's crazy, I know it, and if it hadn't actually happened to me, I'd never believe it. But I feel like I need to finish. At least get it down so that if someone ever finds this, they'll know. They might not believe it, either, but they'd know. And maybe somehow, impossibly, Ma could find out what happened to her remaining kid.

So when the kaiju attacked me, don't know how or why, but I felt this...this *thing* inside of me. In my head. And it wanted to fight them, even though common sense had me trying to run.

But even as I turned to start booking it, a flash of light and a rotten egg scent burst out of me like a giant fart set on fire. I was suddenly covered in dark scales like the monsters and got big—bigger than them—with claws like theirs. I'm one of them but everything on me is bigger than on them, including my wings. I can't exactly see myself to see what my face looks like, but I'm sure it's the same ugly reptilian mug.

Fortunately, once I transformed, I stood a chance against them. But—and this is where it gets even crazier—I could also hear them in my head. Not thoughts exactly, but feelings. Like an old car radio in between channels. Staticky. Louder when I'm near them, quieter when I'm farther away.

The old wizard cursed me somehow, I know it. And that other thing inside me that's not my own mind and not the kaiju, the thing that felt so satisfied when I shifted into one of those creatures, it agrees. When the man threw me into that goo, he cursed me, and I don't know why. But it's the only explanation I can think of for what happened. Guess I have an origin story like Spider-Man, but I'm def no superhero.

I have no clue what's going to happen to me now. Is it possible for me to get home? Am I stuck here forever? When I die, does the curse pass to someone else?

I managed to find the tower he'd been rambling about. Happy it was as secure as he said, plus it's stocked with food and supplies, a couple of greenhouses, and a room full of books. Also, they speak and write English here. Or at least it looks like English to me and I can understand it. But the wizard left everything I'd need like he knew I was coming. Like he'd planned to curse me.

THE DOOR OPENS and I startle, then instinctively hide the book under a stack of others already on the table. I can hardly believe what I read—is this actually a journal or is it some type of fiction? But the details, the emotion, the heartache practically bleed through the page. And all the things that haven't made sense suddenly do.

Victor enters with more food. I realize the light has been steadily falling, and it's nearly too dark to keep reading. I search his sad eyes for some evidence that he's the writer of this journal.

I stare at him so long that he looks up, brows raised.

Then I dip my head, not ready to question him. Could what he's written possibly be true? Is he really the Revoker king? And what do I do if he never lets me leave?

SEVEN

Victor

When I come in with dinner, she's acting weird. Jumpy. Squinting up at me like she's never seen me before. I have no reason to be self-conscious about the scars on my face, and she's never seemed to react to them before, but now she's alternately staring at me and obviously trying to stop herself from staring.

I grit my teeth and set the tray down. The books on the table have shifted around a little. Looks like she's got some good reading done. I've just been painting and thinking—stewing in my own juices, as Ma used to say. God, I miss Ma. But I push that back down to where all my grief and loss lives, in a tiny corner of my mind where I don't have to look at it too much.

"What is it?" I finally ask, when Celena gapes at me for another thirty seconds straight.

She blinks, eyes darting away. "Nothing. I was just…" She waves a hand around vaguely.

What the hell is up with her? I look down at the books stacked in front of her and spot a familiar spine. Leaning over the desk, I pluck my journal from the pile where she'd tried to hide it, anger sparking inside me.

"Wait!" she cries, holding her hands out as if I'm trying to steal her baby.

"This is personal," I say through clenched teeth.

"I didn't know what it was at first. I thought it was just another book but...Is it real? What you wrote? You were brought here from somewhere else? Another world?"

My heartbeat slows and the flare of anger fades. Her eyes are wide and round, disbelieving. Even in a place where monsters roam the earth, being pulled from an alternate universe doesn't seem to be common here.

"It's all true."

"And you really are a Revoker?" Still the disbelief. She looks me up and down, eyes still wide as an anime character, but not with fear. It's curiosity mostly, which isn't what I would have expected. She shakes her head. "That's not how it works, though."

Her brow crinkles, and it's one of the most adorable things I've seen. Whoa. Where the hell did that thought come from? Celena is many things, but adorable? Stubborn, sure. Haughty? Check. I take a deep breath and massage the bridge of my nose.

I pull out a chair and sit across from her. Time to hash this out. "Okay, cards on the table." She tilts her head in confusion and the word adorable comes to mind again. I banish it to the furthest recesses of my brain. "We lay everything out," I explain. She nods.

"I answer your questions truthfully, and you answer mine. Honor system."

Her shoulders straighten. "I am the Nimali princess. My honor is unquestionable."

I hold back a chuckle, figuring she wouldn't appreciate it as earnest as she's being. "Cool. So what exactly is a parallel?"

She purses her lips. "It's a soulsmate." I flinch—that was not what I was expecting—and she starts again patiently. "Here, when you reach the age of maturity, you go through a ceremony using the bliss to travel to the Origin—the spirit world—where a daimon chooses you. The daimons are spirits who want to experience the material world. There, they exist only as pure energy, but when they choose us, we create a covenant and share our bodies with them.

"The Nimali, my clan, use the daimon's magic to shift into physical manifestations of them, which look like animals. There's another clan, the Fai, who are our enemies and don't change their appearance, but take on animal qualities and abilities nevertheless." She frowns like this bothers her.

"Our daimons form bonds with one another in the Origin and sometimes want these relationships to continue in the mortal world. Both bonded partners, or parallels, will choose human hosts who are closely related, usually a parent, sibling, child, close friend, or lover. It's relatively uncommon, but very special."

"How do you know when you've found your parallel?" I ask.

"Your daimon knows. I think...I think you sense it. You can't talk with words to the spirit inside you, but there is a form of communication."

I nod. "Yeah, it's like an extra sense that doesn't belong to you. But it's always there." I rub the center of my chest as if I could touch the thing that's taken up space inside me.

"Listen, Victor. I know you said you think I may be your parallel, but I don't have a daimon. That's why I'm here. I failed my first trial at home. I only have two more opportunities, and I came all this way to do the trial again in a fresh bliss pool. One that hasn't been as overused as the ones back home."

My jaw tenses. "That gooey blue stuff, right?"

She nods.

"Celena, that place is dangerous. There are kaiju—Revokers—all around it all the time. It's—"

"You have no idea how important this is." She leans

forward, her eyes lit up from within. "My people are depending on me to be a good queen. I can help lead them out of the troubles we're in. The war with the Fai needs to end. Our bliss is running out, and my father…"

She takes a deep breath, gathering herself. "My father has made some decisions that are…unwise. But I can change his mind. He'll only respect me, only listen to me if I have a daimon, though. A strong one. I need to be a dragon." The last, she says softer, almost to herself.

"Dragon?" She mentioned her father was a dragon before, but I'd kind of hoped it was a metaphor.

Her lips quirk crookedly. "You've seen the Revokers. You doubt there are dragons?"

I've been here a long time, but I haven't really left Oakland. Seems like I've been missing out. The various people I've met over the years, none of them transformed into creatures of any kind. "The Nimali and the Fai, they don't leave your city very much, do they?"

"The Air Nimali patrol the eastern bay occasionally, but only in their bird forms. Our soldiers monitor the area directly south of the wall, but that's all. We're…safe there," she says.

So the fact that she ventured out alone must have taken an extreme amount of courage. I sit back in my seat, gazing at her through fresh eyes. "What else is there? What other kinds of creatures?"

She shrugs. "Everything else."

"Unicorns, griffins?"

"Phoenixes, cherufes, krakens, wendigos."

My jaw actually drops. "Wait, those are all real?"

"As real as you or me. Not nearly as common as the wolves and bears and crows and sharks and all, but daimons of all kinds create covenants with us." She tilts her head to the side again, watching me. Something behind my rib cage heats and loosens at the same time. I try to ignore it.

"Will you help me?" she asks. "I promise to help you if I can. But there won't be a way to know until I leash a daimon."

"And to do that, you have to go to the…"

"Bliss pool," she finishes.

I wipe a hand down my face, feeling weary. Is this more manipulation? Given how obvious she was at first, trying to pull my strings, if she were capable of being subtle and devious, wouldn't she have brought out the big guns early? Or not. What do I know? My experience with girls was mostly cut off at sixteen, so I'm not some kind of expert.

But her face is open, more so than I've ever seen it, and it's doing strange things to my chest and other parts of my body. I don't think she's lying. She may be proud and mule-headed, but she seems to be sincere as well. She wants to go to that bliss pool—a place I still see in my nightmares. It was terrifying for me, dragged there against my will and tossed in. Then again, I had no idea of what to expect. She knows all about it.

And if it's the only way to be sure if she's my parallel, then I have to do it. I know that.

She's still gazing at me softly, giving me time to wade through my thoughts. God, she's beautiful. I don't want to let myself think about that, but it's hard to bury every single emotion all the time. Beautiful and determined. Passionate about helping her people. There really isn't a decision to make.

I push away from the table to stand. "All right. I'll take you to this bliss pool. But you have to—" My words are swallowed by the rumbling of the ground underfoot. Books slide from their neat piles on the tables and the walls shudder. A crack sounds and then everything starts shaking again.

"Earthquake!" I shout just before the walls cave in.

EIGHT

Celena

THE EARTHQUAKES USED to be much more common. Right after the Sorrows, they were nearly constant. And even when I was a child, the earth would shake and groan weekly with minor events.

Back then, I would ignore the rules and instructions about going into the interior closet to stay safe. Instead, I would run to my mother's suite and climb into her bed. She would press my hair back and sing to me. Hold me in her arms through the aftermath or aftershocks, her skin scented with lavender. That smell brings me comfort to this day; I would give anything to inhale her special mix of it again. I've never been able to recreate it.

Now, fear burns in my belly. Victor shouts as I grip the table with both hands, and the world shudders and shakes around us. Then the shelves along the wall fall apart. The tumbling books are a rockslide. I scream.

We're in the center of the room, so it's maybe a second or two before the avalanche hits me. But Victor is there. He scoops me up and darts out of the way of the deluge headed toward us. We race around the other tables and through the room of shuddering shelving into the bathing room.

It's not the same space I've been using. This one is empty of all its plumbing and equipment. Just blank tiles with holes in the walls where things used to be. But here there's nothing to fall on our heads. It's relatively safe, like the closets I was supposed to hide in as a child.

He slides against the wall with me still tucked into his arms. I should probably complain, but the terror still has me in its grip.

"Are you all right?" He's so close, his breath feathers my ear. My heart races and I take a deep, steadying breath, only to have my lungs filled with his unique scent. Not lavender, but still comforting. Which is illogical, because he is still my captor. Isn't he?

"Celena?" He gives me a little shake, worry evident in his voice.

"I'm okay. I wasn't harmed."

He sighs, sounding relieved, and the limbs wrapped around me relax. "That was a bad one, huh?"

"I hope it's over."

"Me too. What do you think? Five or six on the Richter scale, maybe?"

I have no idea what he's talking about.

"Do you all rate the strength of the earthquakes here?" he asks.

I swallow, thinking back. "The Azure scholars do have some kind of system. But I don't know it. They record it for posterity. They like doing things like that."

"Well, that's the worst one we've had for years. I hope there won't be any more aftershocks. But just in case, we're probably in the best place. Unless the whole building comes down on us."

I twist in his hold to give him an unappreciative glare. He grins. "This place survived the apocalypse. I think it'll be fine."

Finally, I extract myself from him and sit beside him. "Thank you for helping me."

"Sure. I was never trying to hurt you."

Our shoulders are touching. We are definitely sitting too close, so when he slides away, breaking the contact, why does my heart constrict? I really need to gather myself. He may not be an enemy, per se, but…I don't really know what he is.

His fingers fidget with a bit of thread coming from the seam of his trousers. "When I was a kid, my mom loved earthquakes." He chuckles. "She was weird like that. Thunderstorms and earthquakes were her jam. She loved feeling small in the face of nature's might, she used to say." His face gets soft and fond with the memory.

I can't tear my eyes away from his expression. I've never seen him look this way. "She sounds unique," I offer, lamely.

He laughs full out, and the sound expands inside my chest. It's not a sardonic, rueful snicker, but a real, honest laugh. It changes his face yet again. Victor laughing is a spectacular sight. My remaining fear dissolves into mist.

"On nights with bad thunderstorms, she would take us up to the roof of the apartment building we lived in then. There was an awning there that we'd sit under and watch the lightning strike and listen to the thunder rumble the ground. She was never happier." He smiles, but it's sad.

"Us?" I ask softly.

"I had a sister. Sonya. She died when she was young. Cancer."

My chest squeezes. "I'm sorry."

He shrugs.

"My mother returned to the Origin when I was young, too, after an illness." I almost say out loud that she abandoned me, but I shut my lips tight before it can escape. "She didn't have any particular affinity for thunderstorms, but she did love the spring rains. It always made her so upset that we couldn't go out in them because of the fear of Fume Rot. The rain here was poison for a long time after the Sorrows, and after the rain ended, the air still contained toxins. If you got wet or breathed any of it in, your lungs would be damaged and you'd get really painful and unsightly blisters."

I look back toward the door to the main library. "There is no glass in the windows where I'm from. They were all boarded up, and until the past few years, we stayed inside whenever there were even clouds crossing the sky. Which was often."

My life has been very different to his, or at least his in his other world. Which honestly, sounds quite lovely. "That ceiling of yours—to see the sky while it rained. It would have made her so happy." I turn to face him, and he's staring at me, expression strange. I can't quite read it before he blanks his face and looks away.

"Not having natural light must be hard. It causes depression."

I nod. "Those with daimons are helped by their spirits, but yes, it's difficult." The old sorrow threatens to rise in me and I swallow it down.

Victor clears his throat. "I think it's done for now. I'd better start getting things back together."

We both stand and I follow him out. The entire room is in chaos, but only one of the shelves actually fell apart. A mountain of books covers several tables and a good portion of the floor, but the main problem is the only door leading out is blocked by the remains of the broken shelving.

He surveys the damage, hands on his narrow hips. I force myself to do the same instead of just peering at him. He doesn't seem emotional about the destruction. He's assessing, preparing to dive in and make it right. That, in and of itself, is calming. There's a job to do and no one but us to do it.

"It isn't as bad as it could be," I offer.

"No, you're right. But we might not be able to get out of here until tomorrow. Plenty of water in the bathroom, unless the quake messed up my plumbing. But we won't have any food until we get out." He strokes his chin, looking up at the ceiling contemplatively. I watch his long fingers. The stubble on his jaw makes him look a little more dangerous, that plus the scars. There's a strong masculine quality to him that I didn't realize I liked. But I'm drawn to him. I can't keep my gaze away for long.

Fortunately, he doesn't notice.

"Okay, so where do we start?"

He turns to me slowly, eyes comically wide. "We?"

"Is there someone else here you've been holding hostage?" I cross my arms.

His lips curve upward, and it warms me inside. I blink away the strange emotions and push up the sleeves of my oversized shirt.

"All right, princess. Let's make stacks of all the books so we can have a clear path to the door. Then we'll have to get all the broken shelving out of the way."

I nod, appreciating having a plan. Victor eyes me curiously, probably wondering if I'm afraid to get my hands dirty. I may be a princess, but I'll show him that I'm not just here for decoration.

WE'RE FORCED to stop at nightfall since we don't have any of the lighters used for the lanterns. I drink water from the bathroom sink as a way to fight my hunger, but it still gnaws at me, persistent in making itself heard.

After my stomach rumbles for the third time, Victor calls me out. "We'll be out of here tomorrow, so if you have any ideas about cannibalism, princess, just keep that to yourself."

I sputter in outrage as he breaks into laughter. He seems to be entertaining himself quite well at my expense. When it was clear we weren't going to be able to see soon, I settled on the mattress he'd originally pointed out. I'm not sure exactly where he is; the moon isn't out tonight, so it's incredibly dark. However, his voice doesn't sound like he's all the way across the room.

"What do you do when you can't read?" I ask softly.

"Tell stories."

"Really? About what?"

"Whatever. Sometimes I replay stories I've read or ones from movies and television shows. Or just come up with something new."

It's quiet for a long time while I build up the courage to ask. Finally, when my stomach grips itself again tightly and I know I need a distraction, I do it. "Will you...Will you tell me a story?"

"About what, princess?" His voice is plush and kind.

"Anything. Not food, though."

He chuckles. "All right. Lemme think...How about this: Once upon a time, there was a boy named Adom who fell in love with the girl next door. Her name was Evelyn. They'd known each other since they were children and used to make up elaborate games where they could be the heroes, saving their land from the evil wizard who ruled it. Of course, their land really was ruled by an evil wizard who terrified the people, fighting endless wars, forcing every young adult to become a soldier.

"Adom was almost of age to be called into the ranks of the army. But he'd always been sickly, living mostly in his mind and not in his body. Evelyn was afraid of losing him, knowing he wasn't made to be a soldier but would have no choice. So, she came up with a plan to travel to a neighboring land that was rumored to have a magical sword that would give you the ability to overcome evil. Adom, of course, thought this was crazy, but Evelyn was determined and stubborn and so he agreed to go with her.

"One night, they snuck away together to start their journey. Their experiences on the road are a whole 'nother story, but eventually they made it to their destination, sure it would bring them fame and glory and allow them to help their home country.

"But soon after passing through the Withering Wood and crossing the Bogbeast Swamp, they were overtaken by an army of vicious, twisted demons. The two young lovers had no weapons or skill to wield them if they'd had any, but they managed to use their ingenuity to outsmart the demons and hide from them. However, Adom was injured as they fled. He knew he was slowing them down and couldn't bear for Evelyn to get into the demons' clutches. While she slept, he crept out of their hiding place, led the army away from her for a distance until he was captured.

"Evelyn awoke to the victorious roaring of the enemy. Realizing what Adom must have done, she followed the army in secret all the way to the castle where they kept their prisoners. It also happened to be the location of the magical sword, which stood in the courtyard, encased in ice that could only be melted if a petitioner answered three riddles posed by a gnarled crone.

"Knowing she could use the sword to rescue Adom, she approached the woman and faced the riddles. The crone pointed a shriveled finger at her and said, *I contain cities but no buildings, forests but no trees, and lakes, but no water. What am I?*"

Silence reigns for a few long moments. "Victor? Did you fall asleep?"

"Nope."

"Well, what's the answer?"

"You tell me, princess."

"But you're the one telling the story."

He chuckles. "It's a riddle."

I think back through what he said. Cities but no buildings, forests but no trees. What can that be? "I have no idea," I admit, frustrated.

Wherever he is, he shifts his position. He must be on the floor somewhere and that can't be comfortable. "Evelyn thought it through for long minutes before coming up with the answer. *A map.*"

I slap my forehead. I should have thought of that.

"The old crone cackled in delight. The next riddle was: *My appetite will never cease. The more I'm fed, the more I need.*"

Now I know his game. But I still can't figure it out. "I would say me, but that can't be the answer."

"*A fire,* Evelyn responded, confidently. The crone peered at her closely, taking her measure. The final riddle was the most difficult of all. *An infinite currency used by both rich and poor. The more you take, the more you leave behind. What am I?*"

In the silence, my heartbeat sounds so loud. I rack my brain for a few long minutes, wanting to come up with the answer.

"Any ideas?" Victor's voice calls out.

I'm about to give up when it comes to me. "Footsteps! Everyone who walks uses them." I shoot straight up on the mattress and punch my fist in the air.

Victor laughs, though I know he can't see me. "Nice work. So the ice around the sword melted and Evelyn was able to pull it free. She planned to march straight to the dungeon to release the boy she loved; however, the ancient crone had one last nugget to share. *The sword's magic can only be used once, so choose how you wield it wisely.* Then the old woman disappeared.

"Evelyn was stuck. The sword, she knew, was the only thing that could defeat the evil wizard who was subjugating her people. She couldn't both help them and free Adom. She stalked around the castle until she found the barred window to his cell and could talk to him. He understood her terrible choice and told her she was making the right decision by going back home and helping so many people. She vowed that once their land was free, she would return and find a way to save him. And so, they tearfully said their goodbyes, and she traveled back home alone.

"Now Adom, being resourceful and charming, was able to befriend not only his fellow prisoners but also the guards. He had a gift for setting people at ease and folks, even demons, just wanted to open up to him and get their problems off their chests. When the lead guard was promoted, he started giving Adom extra privileges to leave the dungeon and roam about the palace unguarded. They knew he would never try to escape because he was waiting for Evelyn to return. He couldn't risk leaving and missing her when she showed up because demons being demons would definitely kill her.

"Eventually, the guards in the palace led a coup, over-throwing the demon overlord, and the lead guard became their new ruler. He elevated Adom to the position of his trusted advisor, and under Adom's influence, the demons stopped raiding and terrorizing the innocents in the land. Adom knew he was having a positive impact, even if it wasn't on his own home. He'd saved countless lives, but as the years went by, he still longed for Evelyn, certain that she was going to return to him one day.

"Though sometimes, when darkness turned to dawn, and the nocturnal demons slept, he would sneak away to the border of the two lands just to be closer to his beloved. He didn't know why she never returned. He never saw her again, but hoped to be reunited with her in death."

Victor shifts again, the only sound in the quiet space.

"Wait," I say. "That's the end?"

"Yeah, that's the end."

"But it's so sad. Why didn't she come back? What happened? Did she die? Did she free her land from the wizard? That's barely a story, Victor!"

"I didn't write that one. Found it on the shelf. Some stories don't have happy endings, you know." His voice was light, but I caught a hint of something underneath it. Something I had no desire to explore any more.

I turned and grumbled under my breath into the pillow. At least my stomach wasn't growling anymore.

NINE

Victor
_____

THOUGH THE DAMAGE from the earthquake isn't as bad as it could be, it still takes days to dig out completely. Once we make it out of the library, we discover that the building's lobby is completely blocked as well. Most of the second and part of the third floor collapsed entirely, and our only exit from the fortified tower is inaccessible.

"There's no other way out?" Celena asks as we pick our way through the damage.

"No, the other exits were sealed a long time ago to protect from the Revocaters."

"Revokers," she says, rolling her eyes. I remember, it's just fun to tease her and I like how exasperated she gets when she has to correct me. "There was already a hole through the floors here." She points upward. "That must have been a weak point, since nothing else seems to have collapsed in the other parts of the building."

My lips twist. The hole from the first floor up to the roof on the short, six-story part of the building, that was all me. In the early days, I'd shifted in here and busted through all the ceilings straight out into the air. Not my finest moment. I don't mention that to her, though.

Celena is busy considering the rubble blocking the main entry, her lips firmed. I try not to stare at her mouth, but it's tough. She has a great mouth. Full lips that my friend El used to call juicy. I need to focus because thinking about her lips is starting to have an effect on other parts of my body, and I really don't have time for that. Nor do I want to make her uncomfortable around me. Maybe later tonight, when I'm in bed alone and my mind and my hand can wander all they want, imagining anything. Her lips, her neck, her long legs.

I shake my head and refocus.

"All right, where do we start?" she asks.

Celena is strong and unafraid to get her hands dirty. Just like over the past day and a half, we work together well, making a good team. Most of the time, we're quiet, lost in our own thoughts. For me, the drudgery and loneliness that I've been subjected to for years—too many years—is lessened by her presence. Even without talking, having someone else here is nice.

Over the years, I've helped the few people who I've encountered. Some would even stay here for a few days or a couple of weeks at a time. Sometimes it was a good decision, sometimes not. More than one person stole from me, food and supplies mainly. I understood that anyone I came across was in desperate circumstances, so it really wasn't a big deal.

With all the books in the library and all the time on my hands, I'd rigged up a lot of what you might call conveniences. In addition to the greenhouses on the upper levels of this building, I also planted rooftop gardens all over the city and have salvaged and repaired plenty of equipment. If the thieves had asked, I would have happily shared anything they needed. But suspicion and hardship change people. I learned that before I ever got here.

There was also a girl about five years ago. Her name was Bronwyn. She was frail, half-starved like most folks I met, her skin a pale gold, her hair shaved out of convenience. She stayed four months. I was never quite sure if she was here for me or because I offered shelter, warmth, safety, and food—things she'd been without for so long.

I was careful never to pressure her, feeling instinctively that her shy offers to share my bed were more out of gratitude than anything else. But after a couple of months, I gave in. I'd thought…

My throat gets thick when I remember. Well, I didn't think she was my parallel, that's for sure. Hadn't gotten so much as a twinge. It was just loneliness and the craving for a human connection that weakened me. But it was pretty clear sleeping with her was a mistake. She didn't even say goodbye when she left.

Something clatters to the ground behind me. I spin around to find Celena clutching her hand. A stream of blood trickles down her arm toward her elbow. "*Dragon's balls* that was sharp."

I rush over to look at the cut, though with all the blood it's hard to tell how bad it really is. "We need to get that cleaned up. Come on."

I put my arm around her shoulders instinctively and lead her down the hall to the bathroom on this level. The water pumps on the lower floors are usually pretty reliable. And I've gotten good at fixing them up when necessary. Took over a year of trial and error, learning to become an engineer, but having running hot water is one of my biggest achievements.

I'm even more grateful now when I lead her to the sink and run her hand under the spray. While I clean her cut, which isn't very deep—my ability to do stitches is far behind my engineering capabilities—Celena's eyes never leave my face. I feel her stare but do my best to ignore it until I've finished.

"I don't have any Band-Aids."

"Band aids?" she asks, tilting her head.

"Bandages, the sticky kind." She has no idea what I'm talking about, of course. "But there's some fabric we can use."

She pulls her hand out of my grip. "Don't waste it. It's just a minor injury. Nothing to worry about. Look, it's already stopped bleeding."

She's right. She's a pretty fast healer. I still want to bandage it. Infections in a world without antibiotics could be a killer, and while she's not a tiny woman, she's not invincible. But it really is a small cut.

"Thank you," she says and clears her throat. Doesn't seem like that's a thing she's used to saying. But she's still staring at me in that odd, open way.

"What?" I ask, getting self-conscious.

She notches a shoulder. "Just didn't think my captor would care so much about patching me up."

I narrow my eyes. "So I'm still your captor, then?"

"You deny you locked me away in a humid dungeon?" Her brows rise in challenge.

"I think the words you're looking for are 'luxury indoor spa.' And do you deny you acted like a raving lunatic out there and wanted to run headlong back into a pack of Revokers?"

Her eyes darken. "I wasn't acting like a lunatic, I was being strategic. I needed that pack. It has something irreplaceable inside."

A jolt of guilt runs through me. "You don't think your life is irreplaceable?" Her lips part on a gasp. Aaaaand, I'm staring at her lips again. "Listen, I was just protecting you from yourself, princess. You seem to have a way of finding trouble."

"I do not." Her shoulders go back, chin points upward like I've given a grievous insult.

I look significantly at her wound.

"I was lifting debris. I couldn't see it had a sharp edge."

I shrug and turn away, leaving the bathroom. She stomps after me. "Listen, nobody asked you to save me from myself."

"You were literally screaming for help."

That shuts her up. I'm facing away from her so she can't see the smile on my lips. I know I can't have smiled this much in years. Maybe since I got here. It feels so unfamiliar on my face.

"Think it's time for lunch?" I ask. My question is punctuated by the growling of her stomach; I barely hold back a laugh. "Come on, I'll show you the kitchen."

It's weird to feel relieved that she can't run away. If the entry was clear, would she be gone? Or would she wait for me to lead her to that bliss pool she's so intent on getting to? I'm not entirely sure. The idea of her haring off into the remains of this city, where I can't protect her, makes my stomach clench.

We wind our way through halls decorated in the murals that helped me keep my sanity over the years. I've opened up "skylights" at strategic intervals since the second floor has plenty of windows. On the first floor, they'd just be entry points for kaiju, but since the monsters can't fly and don't seem smart enough to climb, natural light can pour in from above.

Celena is enraptured by the art on the walls and floor. I keep thinking she's going to ask me about them, but she never does. And honestly, I'm a little disappointed.

Finally, we make it to what I figure was once an office break room but that I use as a kitchen. It's galley style, with two long counters on either side and a round table at the end. I keep a few potted plants here, right under one of the skylights, mostly herbs. When we enter, Celena goes straight to them.

"Do you have a food production station somewhere?"

"You mean like a farm?"

She wrinkles her nose. "The Fai farm, Nimali produce food. There's a difference." She turns to me. "You just eat the plants the way they grow. Shake the dirt off them and put them into your mouth?" Obviously, this is a distasteful concept to her.

"Well, I wash off the dirt whenever possible."

She shudders. "I could never have imagined eating that way, though...I must admit, it's not nearly as bad as I thought."

I shake my head, starting in on pulling together a salad for lunch while she looks on. "So, what's your food like in the castle?"

"It's not a castle, it's called the Citadel, and it's not wholly unlike this building you call home. Highly fortified against our enemies. Of course, earthquakes do not damage it so easily." She sticks her nose in the air, but I see through her.

"Well, what do you eat in the Citadel?"

"Proper food. Created to enhance the nutrition of the ingredients and maximize the flavor profiles."

"It's made in a lab?"

"Of course."

Now it's my turn to shudder. "And these labs are powered by the blue gooey stuff, bliss?"

She's told me a bit about the energy that powers their world as we've worked. When I'd asked her to light one of the lanterns and she'd claimed not to know how, and been obviously uncomfortable with the idea of fire, I knew something was up.

Imagining a world that seems sort of like back home with functioning cars and lights and heating and cooling—for a minute, I was wistful. But none of the people I've encountered since I've been here have known anything about any of that. And it's pretty clear these Nimali don't care about helping anyone other than themselves.

Celena roams the makeshift kitchen, snooping inside cabinets and drawers. Pretty sure nosiness isn't a princess-like quality, but I don't mention it.

"I fish sometimes, now that fish are back in the water," I

say, "but mostly it's vegetarian." That took some getting used to. Even if there were animals to hunt around here, I wouldn't feel right about it. They'd managed to survive this long and all. The circle of life is a little out of whack here.

Celena hums softly. Once she's done her inspection, she watches me chop vegetables. "Can I…Is there something I can do to help?"

"No, I've got it."

I hand her a plate, and we sit at the table, eating in silence.

The next few days go on like this, digging out, cleaning up, preparing meals. At the end of each day, after we've worked ourselves to exhaustion, we head to the library. I teach her how to light the lanterns and about fire safety. She listens attentively and, though I can tell the spark of the flint lighter scares her, determination pushes her through.

And then we read. Usually separately, but sometimes out loud to each other. I don't see my diary again. Not sure if she reads it when we're not around each other. I always hoped someone would find it—I just assumed I'd be dead by then. But having someone else know me, know what I've been through, it brings a sense of comfort.

One day I find her scribbling with a pencil in a notebook. "What's that?" I ask, coming over to see. She hides the pages from me, looking up accusingly.

"I found this blank book. I'm writing my own journal."

I sit beside her, intrigued. "Can I read it?"

"No." She looks like I've asked to paint her skin green.

"Why not? You've read mine."

She closes the book and places her hands on top of it, affecting a pose of infinite patience. "You should know that there can be…consequences for failing to leash a daimon."

My eyes narrow. "What kind of consequences?"

She motions behind her. Four lanterns light the small area we're using in the library, enough to read without too much eyestrain, but I don't see anything out of the usual.

"I don't cast a shadow."

When she brings it to my attention, I stand up abruptly, making my chair topple behind me. "What. The. Fuck?" She's right. How did I not notice it before? I wave my arm around, watching my own shadow and the place where hers should be.

"I lost my shadow soul the first time I did the daimon trial. If I fail again, I will lose either my memory soul or my voice soul."

I don't think the concept of multiple souls has come up before, and I'm still freaking out about Celena being a vampire. But she's not a vampire, is she? She wants to be a dragon, sure, but other than that, she's just a normal, regular, everyday woman who doesn't happen to have a shadow.

I pick my chair up and right it, then sit. Celena's down-turned mouth tells me that she doesn't miss the fact that I'm sitting a few inches farther away from her than I was before. Then what she said penetrates.

"So if you come back with no daimon inside you, you'll either lose your memory or your voice. Is that how it works?"

She nods. "And if I do a third trial, failure would equal death. You can live without two souls, but not without three."

That makes me lose a few hair follicles, scratching my head to work through it all, but I figure one problem at a time. If she comes back unable to talk or remember anything, I'm certainly not letting her kill herself on a third trial.

She taps her little journal. "I'm recording the important things about my life so that if I forget everything, I'll still be able to complete my mission."

Seems like if she loses her entire memory, she'll have bigger problems than whatever mission it is, and probably so will I.

THE DAY we finally clear the entry and make it to the door is bittersweet. The thought crosses my mind more than once of keeping her locked here with me forever. But of course, I'm not a monster. She'll either get her daimon and we can find out for sure if she's my parallel. Or she won't, and she either won't be able to remember me or anything else about her life or won't be able to speak. Out of all the options, the one that keeps her by my side the way things have been up until now has pretty nonexistent odds.

I take her up to the sixth-floor greenhouse, under the glass ceiling. The panes here represent my first successful attempts at glassmaking, so they're a lot worse than in the library, but still, pride sings in my heart. We're bathed in the light from the setting sun, and Celena looks gilded in gold. So beautiful it breaks my heart.

The moon is already visible, though the sun hasn't quite disappeared yet. I think there's a name for that, but I can't bring it to mind.

"Where you come from, do you have stories about the stars?" she asks.

"Yeah. People have beliefs about what it means to be born under a certain star sign, at certain times of the year. Some think it determines your entire personality."

She tilts her head to the side. "What do you think?"

I shrug. "I never much believed that being a Virgo meant one thing or another. But who can say?" She seems in a thoughtful mood today. "What about you?"

She stares up. "The Nimali don't have many superstitions. We're a practical people. But I've heard that the Fai—"

"Your enemies?"

She frowns. "Yes. They believe in all sorts of strange things. Their religion makes them worship the bliss. They believe it's sentient, like a spirit, though different to daimons. They hate that we use it to power our technology and machinery."

"Everything is energy," I say, thinking back to something I read. "Even plants are sentient. Did you know they can scream?"

Her head whips over, expression scandalized.

"It's true. But it's all part of the circle of life. Things that live can feel pain. Plants gave their lives so that we could have enough energy to get up and do the tasks we need to do. One day we'll die. If we're eaten by something, we'll be returning the favor. If we die of old age in our beds, then our bodies will rot and become fertilizer for the plants who will, essentially, eat us." I spread my hands out.

"That is very smart."

Heat spreads across my cheeks. I focus on the thread coming out of my cargo pants. "I didn't make it up, but thanks."

"Well, you explained it very well."

When I look up, her eyes are focused on my lips, and my chest tightens. I've been noticing her noticing me more and more over the past few days. Her gaze lingering on different parts of me. We're the only two here, so it's not surprising; even so, I grow heated when I consider it.

She's not my captive anymore. The way is clear, so there's no guilt there. But she has a life to get back to. A kingdom that she wants to rule. People who are depending on her. A father who loves her, though from the gems she's dropped, he sounds like a real piece of shit. I have no claim on this beautiful creature. And my life is ruled by this curse, by the creatures I can control and the toll it's taking on me.

"Tomorrow we'll go to your bliss pool," I say. "Now that we can actually get out of here."

Her eyes widen with surprise, and joy, and gratitude. I swallow the lump in my throat. Then Celena launches herself from her seated position, practically tackling me with a hug. I've never seen her so effusive.

I wrap my arms around her and hold her tight. She practically melts against me. Holding her—so warm and soft, smelling sweet even though she doesn't have access to whatever beauty products she normally uses—her natural scent is kind of sugary, and a vast void opens inside my chest.

One more day is all we'll get. Then, in all likelihood, I will have to let her go.

But what if she's my parallel, and she can end this curse—what will happen then? Could I go with her? Be a subject in her queendom when she gets the throne? Be more?

The thoughts turn themselves in circles—a different kind of circle of life. What could my life be like if I actually get to live it? If controlling the kaiju—the Revokers—doesn't kill me?

I don't spend much time thinking about the future; I haven't been sure I'd have one and I'm still not. But if I do, a part of me that I hardly want to acknowledge wants to spend it with the woman still in my arms. Though it makes no sense that she'd want the same.

TEN

Celena

THE EDGES of a dream flitter away as I try my hardest to hold on to them. What little I can recall makes me smile. But the movement of my lips brings my attention to the fact that my face is smashed against something warm and solid and vibrating slightly. Still groggy, I stretch, only to realize that what feels like an iron band is wrapped around my waist. Tilting my head up, the first thing I see are the bristles on Victor's chin.

I close my eyes again. If I'm still dreaming, I really don't want to wake up.

Last night comes back to me in phases. He and I staying up late into the night, sharing stories from our lives, mostly our childhoods. We must have fallen asleep at some point, though I have no recollection of curling up on top of him.

His breathing changes, going from soft and rhythmic to more stilted, indicating he's awake. I brace myself, preparing for him to move me off of him, but he doesn't do it. So I turn slightly into him, sniffing his chest.

"Did you just smell me?" he asks with a smile in his voice.

"What if I did?"

"Can't be that great."

"You smell fine. You do a good job with general hygiene, considering the barbaric way in which you live." I smile to myself when he grunts because, really, I adore his scent. It's manly yet delicate and reminds me of something I haven't been able to put my finger on. I can't get enough of it.

I want to stroke his chest, but even though we fell asleep like this, his arm wrapped around me, banding me against him, it would be inappropriate. Though I feel closer to Victor than I have to anyone in quite a long time, technically I have a fiancé at home.

Shad is my father's protégé and also happens to be my stepbrother, at least in name. He entered the family already an adult, ten years ago, so we never related to one another as brother and sister. The prospect of us marrying has never excited me. However, he leashed a dragon when he was eighteen and is my father's successor. And while we get along well enough, we've never even been friends, let alone more. My heart has never once beat faster thinking of Shad.

Nimali leadership generally passes to those with the most powerful daimon. Whenever possible, that's a dragon; however, if Victor really is a Revoker and can control them in some way…wouldn't he make a better king?

Together, we could truly protect my people and save them from the Revoker threat. That would be worth just about anything.

Shad has never shown any real interest in marrying me. Would Victor be able to best him in honorable combat? Would I want him to? I'm not looking for either of them to die. All I'm after is what's best for my people. And if I could actually marry someone I wanted… Confusion swirls and the warm cloud of happiness that surrounded me when I awoke fades like mist in the sun.

I draw back and sit up, wiping at my face to clear it of drool. "Today is the day," I say, forcing brightness into my voice.

"Yes," he says, sitting up as well. His face is sleep rumpled and adorable and I want to kiss him. That thought shakes me. I blink at him, and he frowns.

"What?"

"Nothing. We should…get started."

He looks at me oddly again, but I stand to escape his scrutiny. My feelings are a little out of control right now. *Pull it together, Celena! Today is the day you leash a daimon.*

VENTURING OUTSIDE AGAIN after being holed up inside Victor's fortress is strange. The fresh air smells bitter to me, the scents on this side of the water different from back home. He leads me across a few empty streets and then toward what looks like a hole in the ground.

"Is this where the wizard man threw you down?" I ask, peering at it from a safe distance away.

"No. This leads to the subway tunnels. Best to travel underground, right?" He says it casually, but fear spikes through me.

He's right, of course, but I also haven't shared with him the weeks I spent in the dark, locked under the earth not knowing if I would ever get out again.

I swallow down my fear, not wanting him to see it, and follow him. The crumbling rubble forms a sort of staircase leading down. Victor stops halfway and opens up the satchel he brought, pulling out a small contraption that he taps a few times and then clicks on. A weak beam of light shoots out of the device. Not bliss powered, obviously, though I can't imagine what its source is.

As we continue to descend, the daylight fades. Soon enough, the only thing lighting our way is the little machine in his hands. It barely cuts through the gloom, and as the darkness folds itself around me, a squeak escapes my lips without my permission. I grip his arm, hard.

"All right?"

"Y-yes. I just tripped," I lie, trying to sound smooth.

"Are you not good in the dark?"

Though I'm trying to control my reaction, I've begun shivering. It's too much to hide, and when he shoots the light toward me, blinding me in the process, he sees it.

"Shit, Celena. What's wrong? We'll go back."

"N-No! I'll be okay. I need to g-get past this."

"We're not going another step until you tell me what's happening."

I take a few deep, calming breaths, and then the story tumbles out of me. How I had been lost for so long in the tunnels with no light except for the glow of the tablet with my mother's messages. The fear and the hunger. I try to stay composed while relaying it, but he must sense my true distress.

"I'm so sorry." Victor pulls me into a hug, pressing me against his chest. I inhale lungfuls of his delicious scent and wrap my arms around him. It feels nice, perfect, like if I had to stay here forever, that would be okay.

My breathing steadies, and I pull my head away from his solid chest. I still have a mission to complete. "I'm okay now, thank you. We can keep going."

His face is in heavy shadow, but I can guess at the expression he wears, wary and almost annoyed but only because he cares. This time he holds my hand and we walk forward together.

Before we left, he brought me a fresh set of clothes, something he said he keeps on hand for the humans he sometimes encounters and helps. "You were swimming in my clothes," he'd said, and though I'd accepted gratefully, I was disappointed to not be wearing his clothing any longer. Though I must admit, these fit much better.

"Scavenging for clothes and other things passes the time," he'd said. "Nothing useful ever goes to waste."

I repeat the line in my head over and over again. *Nothing useful ever goes to waste.* That's what I've been trying to be— useful. To my father, to the Nimali. And leashing a daimon is the only way. Those without daimons can't contribute and get exiled from Nimali territory to live among the few humans who scrabble and likely starve in the unreclaimed part of the city.

Death would be better.

The tunnels here are wide and round, the ceilings so far above my head you could fit a building of several stories down here. Rusted tracks and old subway cars dot the space, some with evidence that they were once used as dwellings, though it looks like long ago.

Every so often, Victor stops and holds up a hand, tilts his head like he hears something. It's something I don't hear, but I follow his lead. He has far more experience out here in the wilds than I do, and I find that I trust him. It would've been funny to have thought such a thing two weeks ago, but now I do. I trust Victor.

It takes about an hour, but he leads me to a set of amaz- ingly intact stairs leading up. We rise back into the daylight in a residential neighborhood, many of the houses with empty eyeholes and gaping mouths where doors and windows used to be. A park at the edge of the block still has part of its chain- link fence intact and nearly pristine. A frame for a swing set rises out of the ground along with other playground equip- ment. It's not all that dissimilar to what I had built on the roof of one of the orphanages where I volunteer back home.

Victor seems surprised when I mention this to him.

"What?" I ask.

"I just…didn't picture you as the volunteering with orphans type."

I grow quiet, retreating at the veiled insult.

"Celena, no listen—I'm sorry." He squeezes my hand, not releasing me when I try to let go. "I didn't mean it like that. I'm sorry," he repeats. "Look at me."

I stubbornly keep my head turned away, but he turns my chin with his finger. "Please." His voice has taken on a singsong quality, and I finally relent and face him.

"I'm not surprised that you give back to others. You're a caring and kind person; that's not what I meant."

"What did you mean, then?" I ask, disappointed that my voice is betraying me by trembling.

"I just meant that I pictured you doing something else. Baking cakes or holding a clothing drive, not actually being in the trenches with anyone. I thought you were kept further from the rabble."

My offense withers. "My father tried to stop me from visiting the children so often. He never could." I stick my chin up, and Victor laughs in response.

"Yeah, that's the stubborn princess I was expecting."

I elbow him in the ribs then point to a large hole in the ground visible just beyond the playground. "What is that?"

"That's where we're going. Be careful." His grip on my hand tightens a fraction as we walk together to the pit's edge. It's like a cave opened in the middle of this neighborhood.

Though at the bottom, only a few feet down really, I spot the blue glimmer of bliss.

ELEVEN

Celena

VICTOR JUMPS down and then shouts that he'll catch me. I'm not convinced, but he insists, so I take the leap, closing my eyes and stepping out over the edge. His arms unerringly pluck me from the air, leaving me with such a sense of safety that it's hard to leave. But I pull myself away, cognizant of what I'm here to do.

Before me is the biggest pool of bliss that I have ever seen. It goes on and on, disappearing into the darkness. My jaw hangs open in awe at the sight.

"This could power Aurum for another decade at least," I say. Instead of gaping at the bliss, Victor watches me. I turn to him, eyes wide, excitement coming from my very pores. He smiles a small smile, then sets his light down.

"So, what do you need to do? Just dive in?"

My lips twitch. "A daimon leashing is a sacred ceremony back home. I do need to submerge myself in the bliss, though I think I'll just step into it. No diving required."

He nods.

"The next time you see me, I'll have a daimon." I hope. The alternative—no voice or no memory—is too much to contemplate. "However, you have my journal if I come back and don't know you. You'll have to give it to me. Hopefully, I'll trust you…" I blink up at him.

"You'd better not fail, Celena." He places his hands on my shoulders, and I think he may lean in to kiss me. Or at least, I hope he will. But instead, he just looks at me seriously. "Good luck."

He drops his hands and steps back. The disappointment is like a tidal wave rising up to crash into me. But I push it away. That's not why I came here.

I square my shoulders and take off my boots. Then slip into the bliss pool.

I take one last look at Victor before holding my breath and submersing my entire body.

I'M WEIGHTLESS. Floating. Bodyless. Composed of just my souls or my spirit or whatever part of me that is connected to the Origin, a place without matter of any kind. The realm of spirit.

It's where we go when we die, where we come from before we're born. It's where the spirits live, the daimons who choose us. I know little about this world, but I've been here before.

There is light. Everywhere, light. Surrounding me like a bright womb.

I exist only as thought, as awareness.

"Hello?" My inner voice echoes as my thoughts reach outward, searching for the one I came to find.

"Hello." The voice that greets me is small, delicate. Neither male nor female; it's not remotely human at all.

"Are you my daimon?" I ask.

"I am *a* daimon. Do you want me to be yours?"

"Are you a dragon?"

It does not answer. My father described his encounter with his daimon to me many times. He spoke of how he felt its vast strength down to the core of his being. How he immediately knew that he had been blessed with a very powerful spirit.

This spirit is cagey and evasive. I don't sense the strength and deep well of power my father told me of. Is it possible that a non-predator daimon would choose me? Horror fills me at the notion.

"Will you tell me what you are?" I try again. My grandfather was a lion, and there have been other mighty predators who have led our people.

But the spirit remains quiet.

"Please. I need a dragon, otherwise I will never be able to change things." My voice is a tiny whisper.

"Is that so?" The voice is contemplative. "Your vast experience and knowledge of the world has told you this?"

I feel chastised and am not sure how to respond.

"Your destiny, Celena, is to unite with a Sentinel and become the queen who is needed to stop the Lost Ones."

It is similar to what Mother told me, though I'm not familiar with those terms. "What are the Lost Ones? And what is a Sentinel?"

My hope begins to sink when I get no reply. Everyone I've ever known who's leashed a daimon has been met with their spirit familiar immediately upon entering the Origin. But this one is barely talking to me and is not at all what I expected.

"Are you still there?"

"Do you want me to be?" is the reply. This particular daimon, whatever it is, seems kind of cheeky.

"Will you help me?"

"You will be required to help yourself, princess."

There is an insistent tug on my body. I feel it from far away, but it shatters my concentration. We cannot breathe in bliss, so these visits to the Origin can only last so long. I will be sent back before my body suffocates, but I can't face it. I can't bear losing another soul.

"If you aren't my daimon, can you please help me find it?" I ask. "Please." But I get no response.

Will it be my memory or my voice? In case it's the first, I hold this tight to my consciousness, praying that I'll be able to recall. *Stop the Lost Ones. Become the queen who is needed.*

Everything my mother said was true, so why is this daimon so evasive? Is it mine or not, and if not, why is my daimon not here to meet me?

Before I get any answers at all, I'm pulled almost violently back into my physical form. I awake to a face hovering over me. Dark coppery hair, brown skin, a smattering of freckles across his face. Old scars that look like something slashed him across the face. His eyes are worried. He's holding me half in a pool of bliss that stretches out all around. It's beautiful, the blue glow of it lighting him up. He's so handsome, but so sad. I reach up to touch his brow.

"Celena? Are you all right?"

The name tickles at my memory. Celena? He means me.

"I'm all right. My name is Celena?"

His eyes widen then close briefly on a long blink as if he's coming to terms with a difficult realization. "Yes, you're Celena. And I'm Victor."

I blink up at him. "Victor. That's a nice name." I smile, and he hefts me fully into his arms, walking me out of the bliss. It doesn't leave us wet, though; it's strange like that. I know that much.

"I can walk," I tell him, though I'm happy enough to be carried. I lean in closer to him and smell him. His scent is delightful, like happiness and strength. Though that doesn't make any sense.

I feel like I should be scared, but how can anyone be scared when they're being carried by someone like Victor? Finally, he sets me down on the rocky edge inside this dark cave.

"I don't...I don't remember anything," I say. But that's not entirely true. There's something that's stuck in my head on repeat. *Stop the Lost Ones. Become the queen who is needed.*

"Am I a queen?" I ask him, brow crinkling.

"Not yet, princess. Not just yet."

"But I will be." I feel that in my bones.

Victor looks pained. He watches me carefully as I look down at my clothes, my arms. I pull at my hair to see what color it is.

"I have to be," I whisper, knowing it's true even if I don't know why.

TWELVE

Victor
___

I THOUGHT SHE WAS DROWNING. She'd been under for so long that I was sure I was going to drag her up and she wouldn't be breathing. I knew that coming to this fucking place was a mistake, but she'd been so adamant. So determined. How could I not have given her the chance to do what she'd come so far to do? But when she sputters and her eyes blink open with no recognition—pain sears me from the inside, burning my chest cavity to a crisp.

Failure was always a possibility, though the whys of it all are still a mystery. And to face losing your shadow, voice, or memory? I can barely decipher the rules of this world. To have her look at me with the same chocolate eyes I woke up staring into this morning, but now blank, a stranger's eyes…I need to stuff the hurt away, ignore the bone-deep ache. She doesn't just not know me; she doesn't know herself.

But she sniffed me—there's that.

I give her some water from my canteen because I sense she's been through a lot, even in such a short time. And the changes that the lack of memory makes in her are subtle but intense. That haughty demeanor is gone. All the trappings of royalty have disappeared, along with her memory soul. But the essence of who she is hasn't changed. Of course it hasn't, how could it? I've never really thought about what's left behind when your memories are gone. Not for a long time, at least.

When I was young, my grandpa had dementia. He'd been a real asshole before, and the lack of memory just made it worse. Sort of like it distilled the essence of his personality to its most basic parts. Without your experiences and your ideas about yourself, who are you? I think it must be the person you are deep inside. And it's just my luck that I meet a girl who actually seems to like me and then she loses her memory completely. It really was too much to hope.

The only thing Celena can recall is that she needs to become queen. But the sad part is, she has no idea what she's meant to be queen of. And neither do I. I barely have any notion of what the Nimali are, not to mention where they are beyond a vague idea of them being in the city to the west. God knows I want to help her, but what can I do?

I'm just about to suggest we head back to the tower, when the sense of Revokers approaching pounds in my head. The awareness of them that lives within me, courtesy of the curse, makes my skin crawl. They're close, and they're on the hunt. With Celena here, ignorant and relying on me, I can't exactly go out and investigate. I'm resolving myself to that when I hear the scream.

It's more like a shout or a war cry, really, but it's undeniably human. This day just keeps getting better and better. Actually, it started off kind of amazing—I should have known then that I was in for it.

Celena's eyes widen. "What was that?"

"Revokers." That seems to ring a bell for her because she recoils, fear clouding her face. I don't know if this kind of amnesia is similar to what I saw in movies back home. Where people know about life and how to do things they did before— they might remember how to drive and play basketball, and even who the president is, but they don't know anything about themselves. Because if she's relying on me too much for knowledge about this world, it'll be the blind leading the blind.

"Someone is in trouble out there and I can help. You stay here."

She snorts, a sound I'm pretty sure I've never heard her make. "No way, Victor. I'm staying close to you."

I roll my eyes, but my chest warms with pleasure. I don't really want her out of my sight. Who knows what she could get up to with no memories?

"You feeling okay?" I ask. She nods. "All right, I'll give you a boost so you can get up there." I point to the ledge of the pit above our heads, then bend, my hands forming a cradle for her foot. I give her a boost and her hands grab at the edge of the asphalt. Then she climbs up fairly gracefully.

I am absolutely not staring at her ass as she makes her way up. Once she's clear, I take a running leap and pull myself out.

The roars of Revokers echo across the faces of the houses, but my sense of them tells me where to go. "Keep up," I announce and then take off at a brisk jog toward the fighting.

It's farther than I thought, near the shore of not-Lake Merritt and pretty close to where I found Celena, actually. Three of the monsters have closed in on a crouched figure. I need to change forms in order to maximize my control over them, but I don't want Celena to see me. She doesn't know what I am yet and even if she did remember, I still wouldn't want the vision of my monster form imprinted in her mind. But the ever-present fog this close to the water isn't enough to hide me.

Suddenly, one of the kaiju moves, revealing their target. What I see stops me cold. It's a bear. A brown bear in the city.

I blink, confused. I've seen some wildlife here, sure. Deer, big cats, a few coyotes, but bears? This particular bear is fast. It spins on its hind legs and claws out at the creatures. The way it moves...

I'm not an expert or anything, but the way it moves makes me think it's not a *bear* bear. Could it be like me? Someone who turns into a bear. Would that make it a Nimali?

Either way, I can't let the Revokers take it out, though I'm aware that if I'm wrong, I might have to face off with an angry man-eater if that thing decides we're on the menu.

"Celena, do you think you can trust me?"

"Yes," she says without hesitation. I don't know what I was expecting, but that's not it.

"Um, all right. Then close your eyes, okay? Please. Don't open them until I come back. And stay right here." The trust in her expression guts me. I park her down next to a rusted-out boxy SUV that reminds me of a Hummer. She crouches and squeezes her eyes shut. I take a second to marvel at her and then back away. To stand in the center of the street and let the beast take my body.

It's definitely the right decision. If she saw me, she'd be afraid. And that trust she's gifting me with based on I don't know what? It would disappear in an instant. But this is the form I can best keep her safe in.

That sulfur smell fills my nose as the black scales explode across my growing body. The wings on my back stretch out, taking up the entire width of the street. I open my mouth and roar just because it feels good. In my mind, I connect with the monsters. They don't want to let their prey go. They're driven by the need to create more of them by killing anyone they encounter. It's primal, but that doesn't make it okay. I exert my mental energy to push them away. Force them to retreat and leave this bear alone.

One Revoker slashes out in anger, raking deadly claws down the bear's side before following my order and moving away. My control is slipping, the thread connecting me to these monsters fraying. A decade ago, they would have left immediately without being able to harm anyone. Now they push and test me like they know how much effort it takes to control them. Like they're waiting for me to fail. It will happen one day. Then, I'm sure, they'll turn around and kill me.

Revoker king, my ass, I'm just a threadbare leash holding back their viciousness. But whatever might happen in the future, it's not going down today. Though they beat against the boundaries of my control, they can't overcome it yet. Grumbling in frustration, they stalk off.

The bear, bleeding, with black poison dripping from its wounds, stands its ground as the Revokers retreat. Then it lets out a whimper and crumbles in a heap. Where it promptly transforms into a woman.

She's injured badly, and I know what kind of damage those claws can create. The scars on my face and body are evidence. I shift in an instant and kneel beside her, searching for any other injuries and finding none. The woman is tall and strongly built, with golden skin and features that speak of Central or South American ancestry, and a thick black braid hanging down her back. Based on her black uniform, she must be some kind of soldier. But the poison in the Revokers' claws is deadly—it's not a battle she can hope to win. Not without help, at least.

I take a deep breath and close my eyes. This is gonna sting like a bitch.

"Celena," I call out, eyes still closed.

"Yes."

"You can come out. And if I pass out and they come back, run."

Then I sink into that same connection I have with the monsters. The three who left still hover at the edge of my awareness, but the poison they secrete is a part of them, and so it's connected to me through this strange bond. I focus on that and push the toxin out of the woman's body.

It's not easy. The best way to describe it is putting toothpaste back into a tube. The going is slow and painful, but at least it's working. I get every drop out of her body—the only way to save her life. The wounds are still there, flesh torn and angry, but that shouldn't kill her. Of course, infection is still a possibility. We need to get her back to the tower to clean and bandage her.

I open my eyes and stand, a little wobbly but with enough strength to hold myself up. I won't be able to carry her, though.

"Victor, are you all right?" Celena asks from somewhere behind me.

My face is covered with sweat. In fact, my whole body is. I rub at my upper lip and my fingers come away with blood. Celena's worried face comes into focus.

"I'm fine. Just tired."

"What did you do?"

The trust is still evident, and I have no idea why. But I grab hold of it like a lifeline. "Saved her life."

She looks down at the unconscious woman, a frown puckering her forehead. "She'll live?"

"She should, but she needs to get cleaned and patched up. We need to take her home. I don't think I can lift her." The world is spinning a bit and black is creeping into the edge of my vision.

"I can help," Celena announces.

Just as she crouches, the woman stirs. Her eyes blink open, revealing brown with flecks of gold. I wait for her to return to reality. When she does, she stares straight at Celena.

"Your Grace?" she croaks, and something catches in my chest. She knows her. Celena tilts her head.

"I'm Zanna, Your Grace. One of K—Prince Shad's guards. I was sent to find you."

Celena smiles. "So, you know me?"

Zanna's brow furrows. She looks over at me, then does a double take, her mouth gaping open and closed.

"She tried for a daimon and came back with no memory," I offer.

Again, Zanna looks from me to Celena and back. "Who are you?" she asks me. Her voice is sharp and accusing with a hint of fear. I freeze. Did she see my shifted form? Does she remember? Is that why she's acting this way?

"This is Victor," Celena says brightly.

Fear doesn't seem to be Zanna's primary emotion, though. Whatever she's feeling, she clamps it down behind a practice wall of blankness.

"Victor Tremblay at your service," I say, giving her a smile that in no way makes it to my eyes. "AKA the person who just saved your life."

The injured woman continues to stare at me as if I have two heads and just announced I'm from Mars. I get that she's wounded and has just been through some things, but she's kind of starting to piss me off. I'm two seconds from passing out, ready to go home, and not sure why she's so full of suspicion.

"How long have you been here, Your Grace?" Zanna asks, never taking her eyes off me.

Celena's eyes widen and she looks at me for an answer. "Couple weeks," I say.

Zanna finally tears her gaze away and moves to stand, biting out soft curses as she does. We're about the same height and she carries herself rigidly upright like a soldier, but I know from experience how much those claw marks hurt. At least we're not going to have to try to haul her back.

"I have a safe place where you can get cleaned up," I tell her.

If her expression is anything to go by, she likes that idea about as much as she did fighting off the Revokers. She's welcome to explore her other options, but she wisely nods and mumbles out a barely audible thanks. Wherever this place is they're from, the people are rude as fuck.

I turn and nearly stumble, but Celena is there placing my

arm around her shoulders, allowing me to lean on her, obviously sensing that I can barely manage it.

Zanna's eyes narrow, cutting into me like lasers, but I ignore her. I'm not sure what she finds more distasteful: that her princess has no memory or that Celena has thrown her lot in with me.

THIRTEEN

Celena

I FEEL LIKE A LIVING GHOST. Flesh and blood, but just a shell of whatever I was before. The things I know are these: My name is Celena. I'm a princess. And I need a daimon to become the queen and help my people. A people I don't even remember. I'm also far from home and only a single soldier was sent after me. What does it all mean?

Not knowing anything about yourself is...odd, to say the least. I can walk and talk. Read the remnants of text on the street signs and buildings we pass. I know that I'm currently far grimier than I prefer and my head itches, crying out for a good scrubbing. Also, the limping man whose arm is draped across my shoulders means something to me.

When he asked if I could trust him, it was clear he did not expect me to say yes. But though I don't know myself, I know that he's important. It's a feeling deep within that demands I pay attention to him.

And when the Revokers were raging, Victor told me to stay put and close my eyes, so I did. But moments later, a new roar sounded, louder and deeper than those of the Revokers. Somehow, I knew it was him. I was sorely tempted to peek and take a look at whatever daimon form he didn't want me to see, but I do trust him, so I did what he asked.

Whatever he did to save Zanna's life left him weak as a kitten. As we walk down the center of the street, dodging detritus and the tall weeds growing from the asphalt, he hobbles along, trying not to lean on me too heavily. Beside us, Zanna's steps are ginger. She presses her hand to her still-bleeding side. Every few moments, she eyes Victor with dislike and suspicion. Another thing I know for certain is that Revoker venom is fatal. She would already be dead if he hadn't saved her, so why is she rewarding him with so much attitude?

He points out the building we're headed to, a sturdy tower, the tallest one still intact here. Maybe because it appears to be one of the older structures in this section of the city. If this is where he lives, it looks like a fortress, an opinion that's upheld when we enter and he barricades the door behind us. A lot of work was done over a long period of time to reinforce the doors and walls, and I take a deep breath once we're safe inside.

He seems stronger now and isn't leaning on me as heavily, though he keeps an arm around me as we go deeper into the building, a fact that warms my chest.

"Let's get you into the kitchen," he says over his shoulder. "I've got a first aid kit there."

Zanna nods, but her gaze darts here and there as if afraid of something waiting around a corner inside this building to ambush us. There's nothing and no one here besides the beautifully crafted paintings that cover the floor, ceiling, and walls. I don't have much time to marvel at it all before we enter the room Victor called the kitchen. Though Zanna makes it here under her own power, her strength is quickly fading. She stumbles into a narrow space, bordered on both sides by cabinets.

"Do you want to sit at the—" Victor starts, but Zanna falls

to one knee, propping herself up with a hand. "The floor is good, too."

As she settles down on her back, her movements jerky, he searches the cabinets for supplies, pulling out a bundle of cloth and a small jar of paste.

"Is that for infections?" I ask.

He nods. "How much can you remember?"

I shrug. "Life things. I can identify objects that I know. I just don't know me. Or anyone else. I don't remember a single thing about my childhood, but I can recall the rules of Catch as Catch Can."

He looks at me blankly.

"The game?"

"I'm not from around here," he mutters, then kneels next to the woman on the ground who appears to have lost consciousness.

"Where are you from?" I ask.

A corner of his lip curls up.

"We've had this conversation before, haven't we?"

His expression saddens, like a light fading out. "We have." He lifts the edge of Zanna's bloodied shirt to reveal the wounds beneath.

"Are we very good friends?" I need to know why his mood shifts pulse inside me like an extra sense. Why I'm so drawn to him. But he doesn't answer. "Are we…more than friends?"

He looks up sharply, face blank. "We just met a few weeks ago." But there's something hiding behind those words and that carefully constructed non-expression. Something I don't pursue because he's so closed off now and busily inspecting Zanna's injuries.

Even without my memory soul, a familiar longing rings inside me like a bell. Part of me does not like him touching another woman, even an unconscious one. That same part craves getting closer to him. To wrap my arms around him and inhale his scent. Have I done that before? Is he being noble by not admitting it? And how must he feel, whatever our relationship was, to have me not remember anything about us?

I swallow, feeling low.

Victor rises and turns on the sink, then sighs deeply when nothing happens. "Must be something with the pump downstairs. I'll be right back." He stalks off into the darkened hallway and I watch him leave. On the ground, Zanna rouses, coughing.

I kneel and offer her a sip from my canteen. She drinks gratefully and then grabs my wrist when I go to move.

"You can't trust him."

I lay a gentle hand on hers. "He's been helping me. He was there when I emerged from the bliss pool. I know my memory is gone, but my instincts are telling me he's trustworthy."

She shakes her head and pales, the motion likely causing her pain. "He's not from here. There are things that have happened since you've left, Your Grace. Inexplicable things. Whoever that man is, we don't know where he came from or what he wants."

Anger flares within me. "*That man* is the only reason you are still alive. He saved your life and you repay him with distrust? I'm unharmed, as you see me. There's nothing wrong with caution, but—"

Footsteps sound in the hallway, interrupting a conversation I instinctively don't want Victor to overhear. He appears in the doorway looking satisfied with himself. "Nothing too serious." When he tries the tap again, water flows out easily. "Now, let's get you cleaned up."

I move away to allow Victor to get close to Zanna, but she evidently wants no help. She snatches the wet cloth and bowl of water that he brings and begins cleaning the gashes on her side herself.

The silence feels weighted and unfriendly. We need a

distraction.

"Zanna, are you familiar with the Lost Ones?" I ask.

She looks up from wrestling with the loose bandages. She really could use help to wrap them around her ribs, but Victor looks on passively, his aid having already been rebuffed. "No, Your Grace. What are those?"

"Something I remember from my time in the Origin. The only memories I have, really. I…I spoke to a daimon that said I need to stop the Lost Ones. I wonder if they're the ones preventing *my* daimon from greeting me."

"You believe your daimon is being prevented from uniting with you?"

I spread my arms. "I don't know. But I've failed twice now." That much is clear by my lack of shadow and memory.

Sweat dots Zanna's forehead, and she pauses her efforts with the bandages. "I have never heard of anything like that, but Akeem would be the one to ask."

"Akeem?"

"Our librarian. He knows or can find answers to just about everything." The act of speaking seems to be draining her energy, but she pushes on. "We must get back as soon as possible, Your Grace. But if it's answers you seek, Akeem may be the only one who has them."

I lean against the wall, considering. Meanwhile, Zanna tries in vain to wrap her wounds. Finally, she sighs and looks to Victor. He raises a brow but doesn't demand she humble herself by asking aloud. Instead, he crouches and swiftly wraps her up, then moves away again.

The soldier's lips are pursed. "You have my gratitude," she grumbles quietly. Victor nods, but rolls his eyes slightly. Then Zanna looks at me with a resigned expression. "There is something else you should know, Your Grace."

She's obviously reluctant to tell me. "What is it?"

"Your father…the king. He's passed to the Origin."

I know I should feel something about that. Grief, probably,

but I have no recollection of the man. "I'm sorry for that. Are the people in great mourning?"

Her eyes are dark, and she shakes her head slowly. "I think the only person who really cared about him was you. Many Nimali are happy to dance on his grave, but King Shad needs you to legitimize his rule."

"King Shad?"

"Your stepbrother. He's a dragon and was just coronated as I left."

Stop the Lost Ones. Become the queen who is needed.

"If he's a dragon, why does his rule need to be legitimized?"

"You two are engaged."

I wrinkle my nose at the thought of being engaged to my stepbrother.

"The situation I left in Aurum is complicated. But rest assured, everyone there will celebrate your safe return."

It's what I want—basically the only memory I have is of that very need, but something doesn't feel right. And I have no way of knowing what it is.

"I'll need a daimon to become queen, won't I?"

Zanna's brow furrows. "I think a live princess—a live queen—is better than even a shifter one," she finally says.

I'm not sure I agree.

"Well, we're not going anywhere until you heal up," I announce. "You'll need to rest."

"I'll be right as the river come morning. I've had worse than this."

Victor's frown says he doubts that, but Zanna has proven herself to be extremely strong and fierce, and not just in her bear form.

"Let us see what tomorrow brings," I say, pushing off the wall. "Is there a more comfortable place she can rest?"

"I'm fine here," she says through gritted teeth.

Victor regards the hard ground on which she lies and then

shrugs. "It's up to you." Then he turns to me. "Are you hungry?"

I shake my head. My mind is restless, my insides churning too much to eat. "Where do I sleep?"

An expression crosses his face too quickly to recognize. "Follow me."

He takes me down the hallway and through a pair of double doors into a fabulous library. I smile up at the shelving and rows and rows of books. I have the strongest sense of déjà vu. Joy lightens my heart and I spin several times, taking it all in. Then I notice Victor smiling softly at my reaction. "I've done this before?"

He just chuckles. I want nothing more than to touch the spines and climb to the upper floors, looking down on the scene below. The urge to investigate all the delicately painted scenes and decorations pulls, but so does exhaustion.

Victor paces to one of the tables in the center of the room, stacked high with books. He plucks a relatively thin volume from the pile. "This is yours. You planned for the possibility of returning with no memory."

When he hands the book to me, our fingers brush and sparks light inside me. He blinks at the contact, and I know I didn't imagine it. I clutch the thin volume to my chest and grab his hand. "I'm sorry I don't remember you. But…" I'm not exactly sure how to put this feeling, this knowledge into words.

"But what?" He leans forward slightly.

I'm still thinking of what I'm trying to say when a giant yawn cracks my face. He chuckles and releases my hand.

"Get some rest, princess." He motions to a bed tucked into an alcove in the corner. "We can figure out the rest tomorrow."

I blink, suddenly sad he's leaving. "Good night, Victor." Though light still shows in the sky, I feel like it's late in the evening.

He sets the lantern down and exits, leaving the door cracked open. I move the light over to the bed and settle onto the mattress. However, tired as I am, the little journal in my hand pulls my attention. I open it to the first page and start to read.

As I flip the pages, my blood turns cold. The looping script that must be my own is a series of hastily written notes to myself. Recollections. Hopes.

My father, King Lyall, features prominently, and what I read lets me know the man is, or rather was, absolutely ruthless. Exacting. Demanding. Unforgiving. And Prince Shad is his protégé. He must be a tyrant as well.

Zanna seems to believe that this Shad wants me back out of concern for my well-being and to add continuity to his rule, but I'm not so sure. My existence as the legitimate daughter of the former king makes me more of a threat to his rule than an aid.

She seemed sincere, and sounded incredibly loyal to the new king, but the only thing that makes sense is that he's planning to have me killed as soon as I step foot back into Aurum. According to the father described in this journal, it seems like something the late king would have taught him. Kill first, ask questions later.

If I'm to be the queen who is needed, then I'll still need to return and face the current king, but I can't do it unprotected. Zanna has showed where her allegiance lies, so I cannot rely on her. And now her distrust of Victor is making more sense. She knows he has some kind of ability to defend against the Revokers. Maybe she's afraid he's more powerful than King Shad.

My only chance of success just might like in convincing Victor to come back with me and help.

I finally get to sleep, but it's restless and racked by dreams of a dragon chasing me through the streets.

FOURTEEN

Victor

In the morning, as I take the familiar steps down the hallway, carrying the same makeshift tray like some kind of dystopian butler, I'm filled with anticipation. I'm no longer Celena's captor, so that issue isn't between us anymore. That's probably the only aspect of her memory loss I don't hate.

I enter the library to find the sleeping alcove empty. Unease rises in my chest. I scan the room, spotting her silhouetted form scanning the shelves high above.

"Find anything good?" I call up to her.

She startles at my voice, almost dropping the book in her hand before catching herself. "Just browsing. Seeing what calls to me."

I set the tray down and climb the ladder to join her, sitting with my back against the wall, watching her skim title after title. Her brow is furrowed in concentration, but underneath is a layer of uncertainty I can't ignore. "What's on your mind, princess?"

Celena meets my gaze, chewing her bottom lip. It's a distracting sight. "I read through my journal last night. And… I'm worried about returning to Aurum."

She sits beside me and recounts what she learned of her

father and his protégé, King Shad. The trepidation in her voice matches the tremor in my gut at the thought of her walking into that kind of situation alone.

"For what it's worth, you never seemed afraid of Shad before. You weren't friends or anything, and you weren't excited about the idea of marrying him, but he didn't sound like the same type of asshole your dad was."

Frustration fills her, and she clenches her fists. "It's hard to know what to think. There's not a lot that I left for myself, just the basics, really. I was wondering…" Celena glances at me before looking away, uncharacteristically shy. "Actually, I was hoping you might come back with us. I'm not sure that I can believe what Zanna is telling me. You're the only one I trust."

Those words from her do something to me. They make feelings come alive inside me that I haven't felt in a long time, maybe never. "What are you thinking?"

She twists her hands in her lap. "I have reason to believe that the journey back will be filled with Revokers. And you have some sort of ability over them, don't you?"

I nod, keeping my mouth pressed shut. After her reaction the first time, I don't want to reveal the truth about my daimon again, but after yesterday she knows I saved Zanna's life somehow.

"I would feel so much better with you there," she says. "I don't know what I'm walking into. Who my allies or my enemies are. I don't know anything at all." And though she stays composed, the turmoil inside her is clear.

"Are you sure you want to go back at all?" The question tumbles out of my mouth before I can stop it. I clench my teeth together to stop from saying anything else stupid.

"I think…or rather, I believe, that people are relying on me. I have a duty."

As I understand it, the only way for her to get her memory back is to join with a daimon. But she only has one attempt left, and if she fails, it will kill her. Then it wouldn't matter if she was my parallel or not. The very idea has me clenching my fists, a tight anger unfurling in my belly. I care about her too much. I want her to live too much, even if it means dooming the world with the unchecked monsters.

If I were a more selfish creature, I'd take her back to the bliss pool right now. Only a successful connection with a daimon can let us know once and for all if she is my parallel. And if she is, we can destroy the Revokers for good. But there's a fifty-fifty chance that another trial will consign her to death. My fists clench and loosen, clench and loosen until Celena places a hand over them, calming me instantly.

I take a deep breath. She was never going to just stay here forever. "My control over them…it isn't complete. It drains me quickly. I'm not sure…" I shake my head, unwilling to admit weakness in front of her, but also unwilling to have her thinking I could do more and I'm simply refusing. "Honestly, it's a miracle that I didn't pass out after we found Zanna. I can't promise perfect control."

I've been wondering about that. My best guess is that I couldn't bear to leave Celena alone with an unknown person, so I used every last bit of energy to stay conscious.

She squeezes my hand gently and smiles. "Perfect control probably isn't possible. But you can give us a chance, at least. Whatever control you do have is rare. At least, I think it is." She frowns.

"I think so, too."

"So, will you come with us?" Sunlight makes her skin seem to glow. The golden gleam filters in through my shoddy glass-work in the ceiling, highlighting the force of Celena's beauty. I find myself just staring at her, not quite sure she's real. She stares right back.

Her hand on mine slides up my arm to my biceps. I'm wearing a short-sleeve shirt today, and her fingertips creep underneath the sleeve, meeting the raised ridges of the scar on my shoulder.

Softly, she caresses my rougher skin. Her face draws nearer until her warm breath brushes against my lips. Is she feeling the same draw as I do? The one that's like a tether between us, connecting us from heart to heart and growing shorter every moment. I lean in, unable to pull away. Unwilling to be even an inch farther from her. With her other hand, she reaches out to trace the scars on my face. I close my eyes. I don't think anyone but me has ever touched them before.

The scent of her skin surrounds me. The feel of her fingers gently stroking the evidence of my pain tightens everything within me. I don't know when my arms go around her, but I pull her closer until she's basically on my lap. Then our lips crash together.

She winds her arms around me, tilting her head, and for a moment, we drown in each other. Her hands grasp my short hair, mine tighten around her waist, dragging her closer, pressing her into me. Her legs wrap around me, and it's like we're trying to fuse ourselves into a new entity. Transform into a creature with four arms and four legs. Our tongues tangle in a kiss made of pure intensity.

I don't want to come up for breath. I don't ever want to be doing anything else again. But the crash of the door slamming open jerks us apart.

"Your Grace?" Zanna's voice from the bottom level cools things between the two of us about a hundred degrees. Fortunately, from where we are on the second level, I don't think she can see us. She's made it pretty clear she hates me, and even if she didn't, Celena's a princess. What royal subject in her right mind would think me an appropriate option?

Celena drops her forehead to mine, breathing heavily. She gives my cheek one last caress, and then she stands. My heartbeat hasn't slowed yet. Darkness creeps into my vision, but I'm not going to pass out. That was definitely the fiercest, most passionate kiss I've ever experienced, not that I've had many, and it's left me reeling.

Whatever Celena says to Zanna doesn't filter through the static in my head. Their voices sound like the adults in a Charlie Brown cartoon as I relive the kiss.

I don't know how parallels work. Celena swore up and down that there's no way to know without a daimon, but I'm now entirely certain this woman is mine. And even if it kills me, I'll protect her till the day I die. I will do everything in my power, Revokers or no, to make sure she's safe.

FIFTEEN

Victor
―――――――

THOUGH ZANNA WANTS to leave immediately, she isn't really in any shape to travel just yet. Of course, she won't listen to reason but finally relents in the face of her princess demanding we stay at least another day.

We use the time to organize and plan. The idea is to take the boat that, according to her notes, Celena had stolen and used to cross the Bay.

Zanna is surprised this is how she left the city. Everyone assumed Celena went over the wall they built to keep the Revokers out. The soldier grumbles under her breath about how had she known, she would have gotten here even faster.

And she's predictably delighted to discover that I'm coming along as well. The night before we leave, I overhear the two of them hissing in an argument. Well, Zanna is doing most of the arguing. Celena listens with an air of angelic patience, only interjecting here and there to defend me.

I know I shouldn't be eavesdropping, but I can't help it. Besides, this is my home. I can stand in any hallway I want... just out of sight...listening in on a conversation not meant for my ears. So I'm a creeper; whatever.

Given the fact that I did save Zanna's life, and I've been

providing her with food and water for the past few days, you'd think she'd get off her high horse. But evidently not.

Whenever she looks at me, she practically shudders, like the very sight of me is revolting. I have no idea what that's all about. For a minute, I consider confronting her, but I don't really want to show my hand. Don't want her to know how little I know about this world. It would only give her more ammunition.

However, Zanna doesn't leave Celena's side, taking it upon herself to guard the woman, so there are no more kisses between the princess and I. It's just as well. I'm leading her back to her home, where she's a royal with countless privileges. Not to mention she has a fiancé waiting for her, who also happens to be the king. And a dragon.

Now, I've never met a dragon, but I'm pretty sure my Revoker form could take him. However, that's not what we're here for. Fighting over Celena won't help her, and it won't help me find my parallel or destroy the kaiju.

I pack up our supplies, enough for a week or so, and then we head out. Celena's notes are kind of vague about the location of the boat. She shows me the journal and I can't make heads or tails of her location descriptors—I'm starting to suspect she has a terrible sense of direction—but I do know where a few other seaworthy boats are stored. Some of the people I've helped over the years have arrived that way, coming across the water from parts north and west, following rumors of a settlement to the east.

We find a little rowboat that looks pretty decent. There are two good-sized oars intact on its bottom, and it doesn't have any visible holes. I've never imagined rowing across the San Francisco Bay before. Then again, I never imagined a lot of what's happened to me in the past twelve years.

The day is overcast and foggy like every day here is. But we set out early enough that even though I have no idea how long it will take to row across the water, I figure we'll get there well before nightfall. What I don't expect is the thunderstorm.

The apocalypse that destroyed this place—the Sorrows, Celena called it—was apparently a mash-up of multiple climate change disasters plus World War III. All of the above affected the weather for the decades afterward. When I first got here, along with the earthquakes rumbling with more frequency than I was used to, the storms were vicious serial killer versions of the thunderstorms back home.

They've gotten less frequent as the Earth heals itself, but when one hits, it's still basically the worst version of any storm I grew up with. So today, when the relatively bright clouds start to darken ominously about a half hour after we start out, I know it's going to be bad.

It's actually worse.

The rain starts as a cold drizzle, which quickly morphs into a driving, lashing downpour. Thunder roars and lightning strikes in the distance. Rowing in conditions like this soon becomes impossible. I can't keep the boat straight, and as the skies darken even more, I lose my sense of direction. I have no idea which way we're even going. The water that started out so placid now rocks violently; we're being soaked from all sides.

"Let me have the oars!" Zanna shouts over the screams of the racing wind.

"If you think you can do better, you're delusional, lady!" I yell back, but I'm exhausted. My muscles are tight and sore, my hands blistered blocks of ice, so I hand them over. Maybe she knows something I don't.

Turns out she doesn't. She makes absolutely no headway against Mother Nature, but I'm too wet and cold to be properly smug about it.

A giant crack splits the air, and the boat starts to vibrate.

"What was that?" Celena yells.

I whip my head around trying to figure that out, but

between the darkened skies and the assaulting rain, it's impossible to see anything. We don't have any light sources with us; there's no point in using the hand-crank flashlight. It will only light up about two inches in front of us. The answer comes when I feel the water start to rise from the bottom of the boat.

"We must have hit something," I announce. "We're taking on water."

Zanna curses up a storm using words I've never even heard before.

"What should we do?" Celena grips my forearm. Her fingers are almost frozen solid and I rub them between my palms.

"I don't know where we are," I admit. "But we need to find land as soon as possible. Or we'll be swimming the rest of the way. I know bears can swim, but can you?"

Celena's eyes are wide. She shakes her head, uncertain. I turn to Zanna, who's just as mystified. "I can't imagine why she'd know how to swim," the woman says. "Once you have a daimon, that form might be able to; otherwise, there's no reason for it."

I figured as much. So it's become doubly important for us to find land. I'd say we should turn back—it must be closer than trying to reach our destination—but as the storm intensifies, the boat seems to be spinning. "Bring the oars in, Zanna. They're not doing any good. We don't want to lose one."

Of course, she doesn't listen to anything I say. She's stubbornly trying to still row in the dark against the waves and the wind.

Another big swell lifts us up, giving me that weightless, belly-swooping sensation like I'm on a roller coaster. When we crash back down, the water seeping into the boat rises faster. I bail it out with my cupped hands; Celena does the same, matching my movements. Then Zanna cries out, her arm wrenching upward.

I watch in dismay as one of the oars goes flying.

My eyes close, and I take a deep breath. If it's possible for this situation to get worse, I don't know how. Even if the storm ended right now, steering the boat with just one oar is impossible.

I squint against the darkness, desperately trying to spot anything that could save us. Could Zanna's bear swim to shore carrying Celena? Of course, even a bear would need to know where she's going and probably isn't so buoyant with an adult woman riding on her back.

Could I fly through this? Carrying Celena? Though the last thing I want is for her to see my monster form, if the choice is between that and letting her drown, there's no option. I'm just getting ready to suggest this when Celena cries out, pointing. I follow the direction of her finger as a strike of lightning in the distance illuminates the sky for a split second.

"Thank you, sweet baby Jesus."

Just ahead, the outline of buildings is clear. Even better, the forces of the wind and the tide are taking us straight there. I have no idea whether this is Oakland, Treasure Island, or San Francisco. We could be in Sausalito for all I care, far off course from our destination. Land is land.

The boat runs aground on the rocky shore, and I grab my pack, then help Celena out. I fish out the flashlight and crank it up. In the pitch darkness, it's a godsend. Once the storm ends and light returns to the world, we'll have to reorient ourselves and figure out exactly where we are. For now, shelter is what we need.

The first building we come across is an abandoned gas station that still has a mostly intact roof and a room with four walls. It smells like a sewer and boasts suspicious stains on the floor, but in my eyes, it's the Ritz.

I WAKE while the women are still asleep and sneak out of the nasty but dry room we slept in. The day has dawned bright and sunny, and the ever-present fog of the city is nowhere to be found. The sky even has the nerve to be blue. I walk a block away, making sure I'm hidden in case either of them woke without my knowledge, then I shift and take to the skies to figure out exactly where we are.

After flying around for a few minutes, it's clear we've ended up in the South Bay, maybe somewhere around Sunnyvale or San Jose in my world.

If I were willing to fly Celena up to the city, we could be there in a couple of hours, but as it is, it'll take days to walk. At least it's more time with her—maybe the last time we'll get together.

I turn, swooping back toward where we spent the night, when my senses fire with warning. Revokers.

Flying toward the sense of them that's lodged itself in my brain, a sick feeling spreads through my gut. I'm perceiving a lot of them, like a *lot*.

They're out west, on the coast south of Half Moon Bay overlooking the ocean. I stay high, relying on the clouds for cover, though none of them can use their wings to get even a foot off the ground. But as the sense of them pounding within me thumps into overdrive, I get a glimpse that horrifies me.

It's like a concert down there. Hundreds, no, probably thousands of Revokers are gathered. They're a writhing swarm. It looks almost like a giant rave. I swoop down lower, abandoning the clouds, my shock and disgust blowing away any sense of caution.

Where did they all come from? And what the hell are they doing here?

As I soar over their heads, several look up, and then more and more. Roars sound. Challenging bellows echo off the sandy cliffs. But while their red eyes flash even in the bright sunlight, I don't sense anger from them. What I'm getting is even worse. A sense of purpose. The kind of clarity that the kaiju I usually encounter don't have.

There's something different about this massive group of monsters. Is this some kind of army getting ready to head north to Aurum? There are enough Revokers here to overwhelm an entire city easily, but they're still far out, and I have no sense if that is truly their purpose.

I head back to where the women are, using the same sheltered spot as before to shift back to human. When I emerge, Zanna stalks toward me from the direction of the gas station. The look on her face is the normal distaste, so she couldn't have seen me transform. But she walks right up to me and crosses her arms aggressively.

"What exactly are you?" she asks, eyes narrowed. "You sound big, and you can fly. Are you a raptor?"

"I don't feel compelled to answer any questions from the peanut gallery." I brush by her, shaking my head because that sounded exactly like Ma. It's something she used to say to me all the time when I was little.

"I have no idea what that means," she says, following me back toward the building. "But my mission is to deliver the princess safely back home. You are an unknown factor, and I don't like it."

I spin around to face her. "And I don't like the suspicion. I've done nothing but help you since I found you and literally saved your life. Now, I don't need thanks or appreciation because apparently you're unable to provide even that much basic human decency. But I certainly don't owe you any answers." With a growl, I turn back and march to the garage.

Celena is just waking up, looking adorably sleepy and rumpled. We share a quiet meal of the rations I brought, and then we're back on the road heading north.

On several occasions, I lead us around a small group of Revokers I sense nearby. Thankfully, not another convocation or whatever was happening out on the coast.

I debate whether to tell the women about what I saw—I don't want to frighten them. Plus, there's nothing any of us can do about the situation at the moment except avoid the creatures. Once we get to Aurum, the leadership there should probably be aware, though I can't imagine how they could prepare if those monsters actually decide to attack.

At night, we find a safe place to camp. Zanna goes bear and sniffs out a basement bomb shelter that looks like it's been used at some point in the recent-ish past. Revokers touch the edge of my senses, maybe a mile away, so it's a good idea to be underground for the night.

On the second day, there's no way to avoid them. We've been on the road for a couple of hours when I hold up a hand and Celena stops walking. Zanna looks ready to complain, but I cut her off.

"There are several scattered groups of Revokers up ahead," I say in a calm tone, trying not to alarm them. "I don't think there's a way to go around them without veering pretty far off course. Just keep walking straight along this road; I'll clear the way and then meet up again."

Questions are forming on the soldier's face, but I ignore her and jog forward.

"Be careful," Celena calls out. I look over my shoulder and wink at her, and then put on some speed.

Fortunately, there's heavier cloud cover today, so I should be able to get airborne without the women getting a good look at me. I shift into my Revoker form behind a building and take off, circling the ladies before shooting into the clouds. Zanna turns, trying to track my movements—she might have gotten a glimpse of me, but I'm pretty fast.

Keeping my senses on alert, I focus on the closest group of Revokers. Forcing them into an action they don't want to do takes a heavy toll on me. But nudging them toward something they want is easy. They haven't picked up on the women yet, and I want to keep it that way, so I nudge them to move west, toward the gathering. It feels like they were headed that way anyway. I just hurry them along. Push a sense of urgency through this cursed connection I have with them.

Once the way is clear, I fly forward a few miles, making sure I didn't miss any of them, then I double back, ending up behind Zanna and Celena. I shift back to human and jog to catch up.

A low-level body ache pulses inside me, and my stomach roils with nausea, but my nose isn't bleeding, and I don't feel like I'm going to collapse.

"Hey!" I call out, running up from behind them. Zanna growls and I'm afraid she's going to shift and maul me, but I just caught her by surprise. Celena smiles, her eyes raking over me, probably checking for injury.

"We're all good," I say.

Zanna's distrustful glare shouts she thinks we're anything but good.

SIXTEEN

Celena

WE REACH the wall on the third day. The others could have gotten there faster—I can tell I've been slowing them down this entire time, but my body is just not used to walking for miles and miles every day. I feel both strong and weak at the same time. Every muscle, joint, and bone aches, and I long for a nice, hot bath. Though I have no memory of actually taking a bath, I know it would be amazing.

After the storm, we had a day of sunshine, but as we traveled farther north, the shroud of fog grew heavier practically each step of the way. The land turned bleaker and was more unforgiving. And several more times, Victor alerted us to the presence of Revokers up ahead and steered us on a wide path around them.

When he's not in earshot, jogging up ahead to investigate a turn in the road, Zanna grumbles that what he does is not natural. "I don't know of *anything* that can sense or control a Revoker like that."

"Aren't you glad he can, though?" is my reply.

I don't tell her what's in my journal. What Victor told me after we met. It wouldn't change her mind about him, anyway.

If he truly is a Revoker shifter, then at least he's on our side and has been helping us avoid the others.

Even without memories, the knowledge I have of the monsters associates them with fear. They're vicious, killing machines who show no mercy and have no higher thinking skills. The fact that Victor turns into one is odd; it doesn't quite sit right in my mind, but I have nothing but intuition to back that up—the same intuition that makes me trust him.

Being so close to him for days and not being able to share more than a brief brush of hands or a few meaning-laden glances has been difficult. My body always seems to arrow itself in his direction, and a deep hollow pit of longing is layered among all my other aches and pains. That on top of not knowing what I'm walking into—having no familiarity with anything but him—my nerves are a mess. I'm being driven forward by this deep-seated knowledge of my duty, but is it enough?

Still, Victor's presence, his nearness, is soothing. And though I'd prefer if his arms were wrapped around me every night, giving me solace, I'll take whatever I can get.

The fog has been so thick for so long that when it suddenly breaks, my breath catches. We step out onto a clear patch of ground beneath overcast skies. No trees or buildings or streets break up the landscape before us. It's just grayish rocky dirt that goes on and on until in the distance it meets…a wall.

"I didn't imagine it would be so big," I say, marveling at the structure that stretches out to the left and right and practically kisses the sky. "How did they build that? And where's the gate?" There aren't any doors or openings visible at all.

"No gate," Zanna responds tersely. "Revokers could break down a gate easily. What they can't do is fly over it or dig underneath it."

Victor seems taken aback as well, or at least I think so. Then he tilts his head to the side as if he's listening, and a frown crinkles his forehead.

Zanna scans the scene. "We need to head to a sentry point. I'll announce myself. Tell them I've located you, and they will let down the ladder. It's the only way in."

I'm shaking my head before she stops talking. "Once you announce yourself, we lose the element of surprise."

She blinks in confusion. "Why would we need to surprise them?"

"I'm not offering myself to your King Shad on a platter." I cross my arms, defiance coming over me.

She crosses her arms as well, mimicking my movement. "He's not *my* King Shad, he's the Nimali king, your betrothed, and there's no reason to sneak up on him, even if you could." She blows out a breath. "This is ridiculous. The patrol will find us eventually, but I'd prefer we get across the wall before we meet any Revokers. They've been very active around here lately."

I look to Victor, who's staring off into the distance, eyes unfocused. "What do you feel?"

"Something's off." He looks around, but there's nothing visible, just this empty wasteland in front of us and a barrier of fog behind us.

Then his eyes widen. "Celena, run! Now!"

Somehow, Zanna both shifts into her bear form and manages to scoop me onto her back. Then she takes off, racing for the wall. I clamp my legs tight around her wide back and dig my hands into her fur, clutching for dear life.

She eats up the distance, the concrete barrier ahead growing closer and closer. Behind us, an unholy roar blares. I recognize it as Victor. It's followed by growls and rumbles, much closer than they should have been. Too many of them.

I don't dare look back. My position is too precarious for much movement. Instead, I hunker down as wind whips across my face while Zanna picks up speed.

SEVENTEEN

Victor

By the time I felt them, it was almost too late. The heavy fog —could it have done something to dampen my senses? They managed to get within a half-mile of Celena; that is unacceptable. And there are at least a dozen of them—a large number to be working together like this. Though based on the gathering I saw the other day, maybe not.

I don't even try to control them, not wanting to exhaust myself this soon while Celena is not in immediate danger. Instead, I rumble out a warning, announcing my displeasure. They call back, no less displeased, but at least they change direction, heading east. Zanna had taken off to the west, so I follow the monsters, needing to ensure they won't remain a threat.

The only thing they could be headed to is the wall, and sure enough, they stop at a section that's been heavily damaged. An enormous crater has been gouged out of it.

I land behind them and move forward cautiously, still not exerting any control but ready to do so when needed. What I see doesn't make any sense.

Three of the creatures use their razor sharp, poison-tipped

talons to dig at the surface of the wall, making the crater even deeper. Their movements are furious, just a blur of arms and claws. At this rate, they'll be through in no time. The nausea that rolls through me now has nothing to do with controlling them—it's rooted in pure fear.

Through the connection, I sense their unwavering intention to get through this concrete block. They dig with a frenzy, changing places every few minutes, like a well-oiled machine. I realize the ones who go out of rotation do so because they've lost their claws. But on their rest breaks, or whatever you'd call it, the deadly tips grow back.

Shaking off my horror, I reach out to try to stop them, but hit a different type of wall—this one is stark refusal. Their resolve is like iron. It would take everything I had to move them off this mission and, even if it worked, it would knock me out, leaving me at their mercy and Celena unprotected.

So, as much as I hate it, I back away and take to the skies.

I locate the women to the west at the base of the wall. I settle down behind them and transform before approaching. Zanna is back in her human form, and the two are arguing yet again.

"I swear to you, Shad does not want to harm you," Zanna is saying.

"And I'm telling you, I don't trust the man. And where are these sentries you spoke of? No one has found us yet; is that because they're planning some kind of ambush? Why *wouldn't* he want to kill me? I'm the only thing that could possibly halt his progress towards my father's throne."

"Listen up," I say, startling both women. Though by now, they're used to me appearing out of nowhere. "About three miles east of here, there are a dozen Revokers digging through the wall."

If the situation wasn't so dire, I would laugh at their twin shocked expressions.

"How is that even possible?" Zanna is thrown. It's a paradigm-shifting thing to have happened. "They've never been able to dig."

"I have no idea. Maybe the digging thing just applied to going down, not through something. I just know what I saw."

Celena looks at me curiously. "Can you sense what they want?"

"They're bound and determined to get through that wall. So determined that I don't think I can sway them off course. But…" I peer off into the distance. "Maybe we can use it."

"What does that mean?" Zanna demands.

"Celena, you want to get inside the city without relying on the new king's hospitality or lack thereof, right?"

Her eyes brighten as understanding takes hold. "And those Revokers are creating a doorway that I could potentially use."

"Are you insane?" Zanna looks back and forth between the two of us, alarmed. "You said a dozen Revokers are trying to get into the city? Do you know the kind of damage they could do?"

"I can't stop them from digging through the wall. But if I harness the desire and motivation, I can redirect it." I'm confident about that even though I know the toll it will take on my body. Allowing them free rein in a city full of people isn't acceptable to me. And if I have to go down stopping them, I will. But I also want to make sure that Celena is taken care of.

"There's a sort of feedback loop that happens when I control them," I explain. "If I give them something they really want, like completing this hole through the wall, then I can have that boomerang back on them and prevent them from actually entering and doing any damage."

Her eyes are narrow as she stares at me, but I can practically see her brain working. "We lose soldiers all the time to them. Do you think you can stop that?"

I hold her eye contact, solemn as the grave. "I've been

protecting people from these monsters for twelve years. Like I said, I don't need thanks or gratitude for doing the right thing. My mama raised me better than that. I'll do whatever I can to protect as many people as I can. But Celena comes first."

She purses her lips; I can tell she's still reluctant. Will she go along with this plan at all? The only other option would be to knock her out to prevent her from shifting, and I'm definitely not doing that.

"I still think this is madness," she says. "But if they're getting through anyway and you believe you can stop them, prevent the destruction and death they will cause, then fine."

We walk along the wall, not encountering anyone, which I can tell Zanna thinks is unusual. Her brow is furrowed, and she scans the territory constantly, likely watching for her people.

I'm still human, but only because the control I'll need to exert when I use the feedback loop is less than normal, and I should be able to handle it in this form. Besides, there's no way to hide what I am out here with just the wall and the dirt.

I stay a few steps in front of the women as we get closer to the kaiju. When several pairs of red eyes focus on us, I connect with them, redirecting their attention to the task and not on anything behind them. It's as easy as a hot knife cutting through butter.

The three at the wall dig faster, urged on by my will and their own desire. They grumble and snarl, sounds that are frightening, but given their emotions, put me in mind of the happy growls a dog makes while chewing on a bone.

According to Zanna, the wall is eight feet thick, and what they've already gouged out is a little tunnel of almost that length. Concrete splinters and cracks around them. I move out of the way of the flying chunks dislodged by the monsters' rapid motion. The hole they are making is tall enough to walk through, an incredible achievement by any standards.

After that, we wait. Celena draws closer but stays behind me as the opening gets larger and larger. Over the shoulders of the monsters, a sliver of light shines through from the other side. The link I have with them vibrates with satisfaction.

I allow them to continue digging until the hole is as wide as my head. Then I tighten my control, taking hold of the pleasure the creatures feel at completing the task and whipping it back on them to force them to move away. To stay on the outside of the wall. To not harm anyone.

They comply, stepping back and forming an aisle for us to walk through. I grab Celena's hand and cautiously step forward, my mind open, confident in my knowledge the Revokers will not attack. They are almost docile under my control. It's as if achieving this feat is everything they ever wanted in life.

I'll have to ponder that later. For now, I don't want either woman too close to them for too long. "Come on. It's all right, I've got them."

Zanna is at our rear, tension pouring off her in waves. Celena also vibrates with nerves or anticipation. Then she squares her shoulders and squeezes my hand, her determination and resolve hardening.

An electric blue glow shines through the break in the wall, reminding me of the bliss pool. Celena releases me and sticks one slender hand through, then an arm. I'm behind her, maintaining ironclad control on the monsters at our backs. They're still meek as lambs.

The cement hole around her crumbles as she pushes on it, becoming larger, big enough for her to stick her head and shoulders through. Debris tumbles away until she can squeeze her entire body through and climb down to the other side.

She's blocking my exit from the tunnel, and when I peer out over her shoulder to see why, my heart stops.

Behind us, the Revokers roar—whether in response to my heightened emotion or to some other trigger, I'm not sure.

They're still in my grip, but their cries are nearly deafening, echoing through eight feet of concrete.

I scrabble to get through the other side to stand next to Celena, the urge to protect her firing harder than ever before. Because waiting to greet us is an enormous blue dragon with an entire army at its back.

EIGHTEEN

Celena

MY FIRST THOUGHT is maybe we should have done it Zanna's way. The dragon before us is massive and looks about two seconds away from turning me to ash me where I stand. Surrounding it are other daimon forms—mostly predators. Wolves, lions, and all types of big cats, along with a few rhinoceroses, and many more creatures, with birds of prey circling overhead. What's more, there are people standing nearby as well, shoulder to shoulder, their eyes glowing blue—Fai. Them being all together is odd. We are enemies of old.

Unless that knowledge is somehow false. Or something recent occurred that was lost with my memory soul and would explain their allyship.

My resolve and my will do not waiver; I must stand strong in the face of all obstacles if I am to become the queen who is needed. This will be the first of many challenges, and if I am to rule, I must prevail. Else, I will deserve whatever terrible fate awaits in the wake of my failure.

Victor is at my side, lending me his strength and calm. And before me, the blue dragon bursts into a blast of bright light and emerges man-sized. He is tall and handsome with short cropped dark hair and canted eyes.

"Celena?" he asks incredulously.

My chin tilts up. "I am Celena." The gathered crowd inhales almost as one. "I have returned to take my crown."

"With Revokers?" asks a tall Fai woman standing incongruously next to the dragon Nimali. She is strong and regal with long locs flowing down to her waist.

"If I must. Are you King Shad?" I ask the man.

He startles. "You don't know me?"

I purse my lips, not relishing having to reveal my weakness but unable to avoid it. "I've lost my memory soul in the second trial, but I will not fail a third time."

Behind Shad stands a smaller green dragon who, at that moment, shifts into a woman. When she moves to the so-called king's other side, my jaw drops.

She's me. Or rather, a version of me with her hair in braided rows. Then another man steps up next to her. Victor.

I look to ensure he's still standing beside me, before turning back to stare. My mouth is dry as I try to swallow.

I'm nudged to the side as Zanna emerges from the tunnel that I'm blocking.

"I think some explanations are in order," she says.

King Shad's gaze snaps to her, relief taking over his face. "Zanna, thank the bliss! What in Origin's name is going on here?"

"I located the princess in the eastern city, as Lady Dominga said. She was with this one." Zanna motions to Victor, then looks to the man across the way, who is his double. The two men continue to stare at each other, Victor's expression full of shock, his twin more curious.

"He has some kind of connection to the Revokers," Zanna continues. "He can control them. I've seen it on several occasions."

The woman with my face calls out, "Victor?"

He snaps his attention to her. "How do you know my name?" I'm wondering the same thing.

"There are many questions that need to be answered," Shad says. "But the first of them is how do you control the Revokers, and how can we trust that you can maintain it? The security of my people—of all the people in this city—is my first priority." His forehead wrinkles with worry.

"It's mine as well," I say.

"Yet you're the one who breached our primary method of protection, allowing our enemy access to the city."

My lips press together, but Victor answers before I can. "They were already digging through the wall. Nothing could have stopped them, not even me. By harnessing their desire, I'm preventing them from entering. But it won't work forever, and there are more of them coming."

I jolt in surprise; he shoots me a look of chagrin. He's been keeping something from me, and I don't like it.

"Let us talk of this in private," Shad says. He speaks quietly to the women on either side of him, then approaches, both of them on his heels along with Victor's double.

"You are all uninjured?" the king asks once he stands directly before us.

Zanna responds. "We're fine."

Shad reaches out and places a hand on her shoulder, squeezing. "I'm glad of it. I'd started to lose hope of you returning."

Everything about his actions and speech seems warm and solicitous. He obviously cares for Zanna, which explains her loyalty to him. What's more, he seems to be a caring person in general. I'd describe his eyes as kind. Could she have been right that he's a good king, not corrupted by my father's influence? Though I can't let my guard down, I'm watchful.

Shad produces a small blue cube and holds it in his hand. Victor eyes it warily. "This ensures we won't be overheard," the king says. "Now, if you please, can you explain all of this?" He motions to the hole in the wall.

Victor briefly sketches his abilities and some of their limitations. How the Revokers couldn't be stopped from their mission at the wall, but he's able to redirect them. "They're amassing. Thousands of them. Maybe thirty miles south of here on the coast, and I think more are arriving. Every one in this entire area, I'd wager. And I don't know what they want, but they're just as purposeful as the ones who were digging through the wall. If they head this way, there's only one way to stop them."

"What is that?" the tall Fai woman asks.

"My parallel." Victor glances at me.

Throughout his explanation, I haven't been able to take my eyes off the woman who shares my face. "Can you explain them?" I ask to no one in particular, pointing to the man and woman mirroring us.

My double responds. "My name is Talia, and this is Ryin. He's Fai, born here." She turns her attention to Victor. "I was brought here several weeks ago from another world. When I died there, a daimon found me and transported me here. It claimed that I was the only one in all the worlds who could be Ryin's parallel." As she speaks, Victor tenses beside me.

"Do you remember me, Victor? Your mother worked for my father for a while. You all stayed in the apartment above the garage."

He blinks, and I see when the recognition hits. "It was just after my sister died." His voice is a whisper.

Ryin's gaze sharpens. "You had a Dove?" Talia places a hand on his arm in comfort. "I, too, had a sister."

Victor and Ryin seem to speak without words, lost in a moment of shared grief. Aside from the scars on Victor's face, they are identical, both lean and sharp-eyed.

Victor turns to me, eyes roaming my face. "Is that why I thought I knew you when we met?"

Had he? Of course, I don't recall. But pain cuts through me as if I've been stabbed by a fiery blade. It nearly makes me stumble. Is this connection I feel for him a lie based only on the familiarity of someone he knew in his old life? I've been trusting only in my intuition. I have nothing else to guide me, but perhaps that was a mistake. Perhaps this whole thing is a mistake.

Tears prick the backs of my eyes, and I force them back. With conscious effort, I face away from Victor and speak to Talia. "Ryin is your parallel?"

She nods.

"And you leashed a daimon, a dragon, on your first try?"

"Yes."

They're holding hands now, presenting a united front. But Talia still seems interested in Victor. "How did you come to be here?" she asks.

He takes a deep breath. "Same story. I was shot in a drive-by. I remember the hospital and flatlining—I think—then I was here. The Revokers found me, did this." He points to his cheek.

"How are you alive?" Ryin asks.

Victor shrugs. "There was a man there. I think he was controlling the Revokers before me. He dragged me into an underground pool of bliss and then I guess I met a daimon. I came out with nothing but scars and a monster inside of me. And the old man died."

Ryin frowns. So does Shad. "I've never heard of a daimon that can control the Revokers," the king says.

Zanna shifts on her feet. "Princess Celena wants to talk to Akeem. He may be able to find out something about this situation, too."

Her distrust of Victor is starting to make more sense. "You knew about Ryin, didn't you? Before you set out to find me?" I ask her.

"Yes. I figured he must be from wherever she's from." She juts her chin at Talia.

"Are there others like us?" Victor asks.

Talia shakes her head. "Not that I've found. But maybe."

Then she looks back and forth from him to me. It's like she wants to say something, but changes her mind.

As astonishing as this situation is, I will need to contemplate it later. "I do need to speak with Akeem," I announce. "I recall my time in the Origin during my last trial. A daimon there gave me information that I need to look into."

"*A* daimon. Not yours?" the Fai woman, who hasn't yet given her name, asks.

"It was not a dragon. That is what I'm destined to be."

Expressions ranging from surprise to pity meet me, causing me to clench my jaw. I can't stand condescension, but at present I don't have any leverage. I must speak with the librarian, get answers, then claim a daimon. After that, there will be no place for this pity.

Zanna scans our surroundings, taking in all the soldiers from the two clans who are still here—a mass of them gathered to meet the Revoker threat. "What exactly is happening here?" she asks.

Shad wipes a hand down his face, appearing weary. Now that I'm paying more attention, there is exhaustion etched onto his face, onto everyone's face.

"A lot has changed since you went on your mission, Zan." He swallows.

"I can see that," she says wryly. "You made a treaty with the Fai, I take it." She glances at the two Fai who the Nimali king chose to include in this conversation.

"We managed to find some common ground," he replies.

The Fai woman smiles for the first time and looks at Shad with affection and…heat. She places a hand on his back in a gesture both tender and proprietary. However, I don't have the opportunity to ponder this further, because the gathered soldiers begin to shift out of the way as a taller form steps through the crowd.

Shad looks over his shoulder. "There's still a lot we need to discuss, but if you want to talk to Akeem, here he comes."

NINETEEN

Celena

AKEEM IS...NOT what I was expecting. Though I can't say exactly what I was expecting. An aged scholar with a long gray beard? A bespectacled youth with skin pale as paper from being cloistered in the library day and night? Certainly not a gray pygmy elephant who opens his mouth and speaks.

"I am so grateful that you have returned unharmed, Your Grace," he announces in a bottomless voice.

I stumble backward, as does Victor. Without memories, my knowledge of the world is admittedly spotty. But I thought I understood the basics—language, how babies are made, how daimons function. And Nimali daimons in their animal form cannot speak. Except that Akeem can.

He executes a graceful bow with his forelegs stretched and his trunk rising into the air. His small tusks are very white, and his voice rumbles across the ground through my feet and up into my bones.

Any idea I had of trying to act regal flees as all thoughts exit my mind. "You can speak." My eyes widen as I realize I may have given some offense. But Akeem merely chuckles.

"The covenant struck with my daimon is different than

most. I remain in this form at all times, and it has gifted me the power of speech so it can remain and observe."

I nod, though I don't truly understand. Akeem glances from me to Victor and a light warms his dark eyes. "This day has proven surprising indeed."

While I gather my composure, the others give Akeem an abbreviated version of events, including how two sets of identical people came to be in this city, and how this time the real Celena has returned and really doesn't have a memory. Apparently, when Talia first arrived, she pretended to be me with no memory soul in order to survive.

"Shad saved my life," Talia says to me as the others fill Akeem in. It's like she can tell I don't trust the king and is trying to change my mind. Looking at her, speaking to her is still surreal. I suppose it will so be for a long while.

"If you leashed a dragon daimon on your first trial," I say, voicing something that's been bothering me, "did you take the daimon meant for me?"

Instead of reacting with anger, she gives me a pitying look, which is worse. "I was brought here by *my* daimon because it and Ryin's are parallels. It chose me. I don't know why it couldn't have been you."

My jaw clenches, teeth grinding together as I prevent myself from challenging her further.

"It is true," Akeem says, reminding me that the others are still close by. "One cannot steal a daimon meant for another. The spirits are deeply attuned to us. They do not make mistakes."

Does that mean that my daimon is purposefully avoiding me? I close my eyes briefly to push past the question, and when I open them, I focus on Akeem.

"While in the Origin, I encountered a daimon who told me that my destiny is to unite with something it called a Sentinel and become the queen who is needed to stop the Lost

Ones. But I did not know what either of those things were—and I must have still had my memories then."

I cannot say whether I've ever contemplated what a frown looks like on the face of an elephant, but I get the sensation that's what Akeem is doing. He glances toward Shad, who appears just as puzzled.

"These terms are not familiar to me," the librarian says.

"Do you think…" Shad begins.

Akeem's trunk curls up to scratch his head. "Perhaps. Yes, that is the best option."

I look back and forth between the two of them. They must know one another quite well to be able to communicate in such a way where words are barely necessary.

Shad addresses me. "Akeem will research these terms and what they mean."

"Can I do the research? Or can I help in some way?"

A cloud crosses the king's face. "Unfortunately, no."

"Why, may I ask, not?" I'm getting the distinct impression that it's not simply my lack of research skills or memory that's the issue here.

Shad lifts his chin. "There are resources at our disposal that are only accessible by a limited few."

Anger flares within me. I take a step forward. "Am I not meant to be the queen of the Nimali?" My voice is low. "My father's death, my *true* father, puts me first in line for the throne. While my absence prevented me from claiming my birthright, I am here now and I should have access to everything."

The Fai woman next to Shad takes a step forward, menace clear in eyes that begin glowing blue as her daimon joins her. But Shad holds her back with a hand on her arm. "Xipporah," he warns. So that's her name.

"This situation is complex, as I'm sure you well know," he says to me. "Your father intended for us to marry, but that is no longer an option. Xipporah here is my betrothed. Our daimons have chosen each other."

I'd guessed at something along those lines, but the confirmation causes a weight to slide off my chest. The presence of the Fai soldiers here makes more sense.

"As for being queen," he continues, "it has never been my intention to deny you your birthright, but you must admit it would be difficult to rule without a memory." The words spoken so kindly cut all the more deeply.

"I *will* leash a dragon daimon. Do not fear."

His mouth turns down. "Be that as it may, you do not have a daimon of any kind yet and you have not been coronated. I have. As such, I cannot allow you to access all the clan's resources."

"Your Grace," Akeem rumbles, "it is not personal. I did not allow your father access, either."

I turn to him, my jaw dropping. "Why not?"

"Because he was cruel and would have used what he learned to further harm our people." The statement is said simply and without emotion but rings inside of me like a bell.

I almost cannot believe he has the gall to say this to me. "I am not my father. But I suppose you have given this usurper access?" I motion to Shad.

"King Shad has earned my trust."

My fists clench so tight they're almost painful.

Shad's voice is still maddeningly gentle. "Celena, you arrived with a squadron of Revokers and a man hailing from another world who can control them. None of us knows your true motives or what any of you are capable of."

I open my mouth, then close it again, rage and fear burning within. "Are you planning to imprison me?"

Shad rears back in surprise. "No, of course not."

"Well, if you think I'm so dangerous, maybe that would be prudent." I don't know why I'm being petulant, but I hate everything about this.

Xipporah, who still holds her daimon, growls softly. Shad exhales as if deflating before my eyes. "No one will take your freedom, but until we know your heart better, until we can trust you, it's simply too dangerous to allow you to access this…resource."

"It's in the library?" I ask, but they don't answer.

I feel like stomping my foot in frustration or having a tantrum like a child would. But the very urge to do such things stops me short. That sounds too much like something a tyrant like my father might have done. I breathe deeply, trying to calm the rage and pain inside.

I want to rule. Not for power's sake, but because the only thing I know about myself is that I'm meant to improve the lives of my people. Shad claims to have the same goal, but how can I just trust his word? Yet he has control. And I don't even know my allies or my other enemies yet.

Those listening to our back and forth all appear to view me with pity. Only Victor shows a healthy anger at the disrespect with which I'm being treated.

I tilt my chin up. "Fine," I say, seething. "See what answers you can acquire. But if you get nothing, we will have another conversation about this and it will go very differently."

My threats are, of course, empty. Shad is a dragon, the most powerful daimon there is. I am a human, down to a single soul. But my motivation churns inside me like an engine. I'm not giving up, and this setback is not going to stop me.

"I will return with answers as soon as I am able," Akeem says before bowing again and lumbering off.

As the crowd splits apart once more to allow him passage, I spot a slim figure with her arms crossed regarding us coolly. Her gaze skates over Talia, Ryin, Zanna, Shad, and Xipporah, and she does not appear pleased. Then she looks at me.

Recognition lights within me, though without any memory

to guide the sensation, it's just a soft sparking thing. I know her, but I don't.

"Who is that?" I ask as she approaches.

Xipporah rolls her eyes and banks her daimon. No one else looks pleased at the woman's arrival. "That is Lady Dominga," Shad finally says.

She approaches, her lithe form small, her bearing regal. She doesn't bow or show any deference whatsoever to the king, which makes me like her instantly.

"So it's true then," she says in a voice like icy water. "You've gone and lost your memory soul for real this time?"

I try to match her posture, but my spine doesn't seem to get that straight. "It's true."

She looks me up and down, then squints at my face, studying me closely. Apparently satisfied by whatever she's found, she leans back. "I warned you it wouldn't work." Then she turns to face Shad. "Word is spreading about her return. The people want to see her."

It's slightly annoying that she's not talking to me, but her statement kindles something within. The people, *my* people, they're the key! Their reaction to me can help. If King Shad truly is a vicious ruler, beneath this veneer of warmth and care, then they will surely let me know.

"I would like to see them," I announce. "Reassure them as to my safety."

Shad glances at Xipporah for a moment before nodding. "Very well. It might as well happen now while we're waiting for Akeem to return."

"I will take her," Lady Dominga says, still not looking at me. Her gaze is so forcefully turned away from me I wonder why she's even offering.

"We will all go," Shad says, the weariness back in his voice. "There's still much to do."

When I start to move away, Victor grabs my hand. "I need

to stay near the wall in order to maintain my control over them."

He's looking a little gray, and sweat has broken out on his forehead. The effort of keeping the Revokers outside of the city must be starting to tax him. I wonder if the others have noticed?

"Proximity is involved?" Ryin asks.

"Yes."

"What else do you need?" Shad asks, appearing concerned.

"Food. Rest."

Shad squeezes the little blue cube, which had kept our conversation private thus far, disengaging it, and gives orders to a group of nearby soldiers to find food for Victor.

I'm torn. I don't want to leave him behind. Not only is Victor the only ally I'm aware of, but being away from him just feels wrong. Is that an intuition I can trust, or should I be fighting against it?

The deep certainty that has been guiding me thus far has taken a severe hit. Is this all just a foolish errand? Am I being too bullheaded? And if I give up, what becomes of me then?

"It's all right," Victor says low in my ear. "Your people care about you. If rumors are already spreading about your return, then the king can't do anything to you immediately. It would be too suspicious. I'll be fine here."

That makes sense. However, I wish I could kiss him. Or at least wrap my arms around him. But that would give too much away. I need to play our relationship closer to my chest so that he can't be used against me by my enemies.

So I leave him at the wall, surrounded by several squadrons of soldiers. I force myself not to look back, though every step away from him is like walking on hot coals.

TWENTY

Celena

"WHERE EXACTLY ARE WE GOING?" I ask as our small group heads north, leaving the wall and all the gathered soldiers behind.

"A great deal has happened during your disappearance, Celena," Shad says, and I wonder about the shadows in his eyes. "Do you remember the Citadel?"

I rack my brain, but nothing comes to mind, so I shake my head.

"It's just as well. It was the center of Nimali life in the city, a fortress where many of us lived and worked. And this morning it was destroyed."

I do a double take at him. "Destroyed? How many casualties?"

"There were no deaths. And most of the injured were tended to by Fai healers. Except for those who would not accept them."

My mind reels, though I don't fully understand the implications of such a thing. "And the perpetrators?"

"Either dead or imprisoned. We're heading to a place where the refugees have been seeking shelter. A great deal of cleanup and rebuilding will have to happen. Now is an inflection point for our people." His gaze at me is significant, and I consider the weight of what he's revealed.

An important part of life for our people is gone now. The fact that it was purposefully done speaks of unrest. Was it rebellion against Shad's rule? Are the people awaiting my return to lead them out of his domination? He would never admit such to me, and it could just as easily be some other enemy who's attacked us.

Since I have no recollection of what the Citadel even is, I'm at an enormous disadvantage. What I'll need to do is gather information so that when I leash a daimon and my memories return, I can look at the bigger picture.

Up ahead, a row of vehicles waits and our group separates, climbing into two of them. I'm surprised to find that Shad is driving himself. Shouldn't a king have someone else handling such tasks?

We're accompanied by shifted soldiers sweeping the path ahead: a leopard, a cheetah, and a vulture soaring overhead, though I have no doubt those within the vehicles are uniquely able to defend themselves if necessary. All except for me.

Our destination is a large indoor arena, remarkably intact given the evidence of destruction in the buildings we pass on the way. The facade is a curving arch, and as we park and exit the vehicles, the noise of hundreds or perhaps thousands inside greets us. We make our way to the entrance to find organized chaos within.

Rings of seating surround an open area, though most of the chairs are gone. The main space where, perhaps in the days before the Sorrows, events of some kind took place, are now taken up by stations set to deliver food, clothing, and supplies to lines of waiting people.

Children play raucously in the aisles as if they don't have a care in the world. However, many of the adults appear shell-shocked. A good number of them are covered in dirt and grime, and it's obvious they've been through an ordeal of some kind.

My sense of purpose coalesces. These are my people. Here are those for whom I've been doing all of this. Though I remember not a one of them.

As we step through the main doors, ripples go through the crowd as people take notice. Shad is an imposing figure with his height and the breadth of his shoulders. Next to him, Xipporah, with her flowing hair and warrior's attitude, is equally as fearsome. They fit together and look appropriately regal.

For the first time, I consider my appearance, caked with the dust of the road from days of travel. Perhaps I should have asked for time to freshen up and a change of clothing before meeting the public. Then again, being relatable could also be a good strategy. At this moment, I am no different to them—without a home and down to very few resources.

I stand between Talia and Shad, and as gazes bounce between two identical women and then to the king, murmurs rise. Into the growing babble of voices, Shad speaks, instantly silencing them.

"Nimali! I know that rumors have already begun circulating. Often such tales offer only the smallest glimpses of truth, but I'm overjoyed to announce that our beloved Princess Celena has returned safe and sound. However, this time she really has lost her memory soul."

Soft chuckles ripple through the audience. Beside me, Talia wears a subtle smile.

"She has been on a journey to reach us," Shad continues, "and while I don't want her to be overwhelmed, given the events of the past days and this morning in particular, you all deserve to greet your princess."

I try to release the annoyance of being referred to as the princess and not the queen, though without any sort of coronation, it is unquestionably true. So I square my shoulders and smile at the crowd gaping at me.

There's a moment of silent confusion, and then waves of people rush forward to greet me. Black-clad soldiers appear, practically from out of thin air, to prevent me from being trampled as I'm surrounded by teary-eyed citizens with many hands stretching out to grab me. I squeeze those I can reach and accept words of welcome and sentiments of gratitude for my safety and health.

Shad and the others step back, allowing me to receive the adoration of the people, who practically carry me out in a tide of bodies.

My heart sings. My instincts have not led me completely astray; if this reaction is anything to go by, I am right where I belong. It is my duty to take care of these people, to help ensure they have better lives.

Time blurs. I'm a little overwhelmed, to be honest. I make an entire circuit around the arena, greeting people and being welcomed back before returning to the entrance where some very lofty-looking Cardinals have gathered, most of them elders. Shad introduces them to me as the king's Council.

Dominga steps forward as I meet the councilors, putting me in mind of a bodyguard. Though she did not accompany me on my tour of this arena and still doesn't speak directly to me, she exudes a protective energy that I find oddly comforting. My intuition tells me she is one of my allies. Perhaps my greatest one, besides Victor.

"Another princess with no memory soul," sniffs a woman who appears in her forties with a straight fall of jet black hair.

"Now Lady Linh," says an elderly man with white hair. "We do not yet know what calamities Princess Celena may have encountered."

"Does *she?*" the woman replies coldly. "Are we not allowed to question her?" She turns to me. "Do you even know what happened to you?"

Dominga vibrates with rage, and my anger flares just as strong. From what I wrote in my journal, I know enough of what happened, but I feel no compunction to answer this woman's questions. So I simply cross my arms and turn away from her.

"Is it true you arrived with an army of Revokers?" asks the youngest councilor present, a brown-skinned woman with a shock of unregulated, coiling hair.

"It was not an army," I reply. "My allies and I decided to use a strategic means to control the Revokers. Even now, my companion protects the city from their scourge."

"I should hope so since you were the one who let them in," the woman replies, direct, but not cold or cruel.

I grit my teeth but don't believe it's in my best interest to squabble with this person.

"What I want to know," says a middle-aged man with dark hair and obsidian eyes, "is if you're here to throw us into further disarray. Shadrach has proven himself to be an able king, and our new alliance with the Fai means that your marriage contract is at an end. What are your plans?"

The question cuts right to the heart of things. Though the people welcome me with open arms, these councilors, no doubt chosen from among the elite, distrust me. They believe I arrived with a legion of Revokers at my back and am here to conquer. Like my father. Suspicion and doubt shadow their gazes.

I don't know how to respond to that, but Dominga saves me. "How dare you question your princess like this? Only hours ago, you had no confidence in King Shad. Now Celena comes under your scrutiny?" Her expression sharpens. "Don't forget a thorough investigation of those in league with the traitors who destroyed our Citadel has yet to take place. None of you has leeway or the security enough to throw stones at others. The only one we know wasn't involved is her."

Almost to a one, the councilors react with indignation,

their backs snapping straight, their lips opening to spew protests and declarations of loyalty.

Dominga grabs me by the arm and marches away, stopping in a quiet corner away from the fray. "You cannot allow them to disrespect you like that," she says to the air in front of her.

I shrug. "They're not wrong. Until I leash a daimon powerful enough to challenge Shad, I'm just an interloper here. And even then..." I look at the well-oiled machine of this refugee operation. If the Citadel was just destroyed today, how is this all so put together already? Shad seems to be meeting the people's needs just fine.

She turns to me, her eyes aflame. "You have more right to be here than anyone. Certainly than any of these scheming bootlickers. I don't know what happened to you out there, but the Celena I know did not doubt herself. She knew her place in the world, and she was willing to take it by any means necessary. If you still want to rule, that is who you will have to become."

"If I still want to rule," I mutter. From moment to moment, my confidence ebbs and flows. What do I want? And how am I to even know when I barely know who I am at all?

TWENTY-ONE

Victor

_____

I sit with my back against the wall about a dozen feet away from the jagged hole interrupting its solid surface. From the bombastic side-eye I keep getting, every single person holds me personally responsible for the existence of said hole. Sure, Celena came through it first, but she's not here right now, so the blame sits squarely on my shoulders.

Fortunately, at least for them, they're able to take part in this epic-but-silent campaign of censure while also working to patch the breach. An assembly line has convened rapidly with construction equipment to fill in the damage and repair the wall.

It must make them feel better, so at the moment there's no reason to tell them it's useless.

As fast as those Revokers clawed through eight feet of futuristic concrete, or whatever this thing is made of, the first time, this patch job will only hold them up for a few extra minutes—maybe time enough for more people to get away.

The monsters push against my control, testing the boundaries. I'm still able to use the boomerang effect to keep them on the other side, but it's slowly wearying me, and their desires are morphing and changing. Into what, I'm not sure. But it won't be long before I'll need to exert even more control, and my body already feels like it's starting to break down.

I can buy some time by shifting in my other form, but how much?

My head feels too heavy for my neck. I lean against the rough concrete to stare at the cloud-covered sky. What time is it? I've lost track completely. How long has Celena been gone? Will she find what she's looking for here? Those answers she's so desperate for?

Footsteps approach, crunching over gravel. With effort, I lower my head to find Ryin standing before me. He's still for a few seconds, as if considering, before sliding down to sit beside me.

There was a time when, as a kid, I wondered what it would be like to have a twin. These twin brothers down the block from where we lived when I was in elementary school, Nahir and Rihan, were inseparable. They'd do everything together and got in trouble all the time for switching places. My baby sister was way too young to even play with at the time, and I'd longed to be that close to someone else.

Looking at my face on another person brings some of those feelings back and opens up an ache in my chest.

He doesn't speak for a few minutes. We sit in companionable silence as the hustle and bustle occurs around us: people carting off rubble, others mixing some kind of cement solution.

"Will you tell me about your sister?" Ryin asks.

It's not what I expect him to say. "Her name was Sonya," I reply. Her memory isn't ever far from me, just like thoughts of my mother. "She was a regular little kid. Loved dancing and dolls and anything with sugar in it. Dragged this ridiculous stuffed pig everywhere she went for years. Made me have tea parties with her all the time." I shake my head as the memories flow back. "What was your sister's name?"

"Dove. She is gone, along with my parents."

"When I left, Ma was still alive. Though losing both of her kids…" Tears prick the back of my eyes thinking about my poor mother. What she must have gone through these past twelve years. I clear my throat. "Sonya died when she was ten years old. An aggressive form of leukemia."

Ryin winces and leans his head back against the wall. "Here, that kind of disease can be healed." He holds up his hands, then turns them as if his mere hands could do the job. And what do I know, maybe they can?

"And Dove?" I ask.

He drops his hands as his lips twist in a scowl. "The former king killed her while in his dragon form."

I shiver at the venom in his voice. "Shit. I'm sorry." I try to imagine King Shad doing such a thing, but can't. "And you trust this current king?"

"He's a good man." Ryin turns toward me. Sitting so close, his gaze feels particularly invasive.

I wipe a hand across my forehead and it comes back covered in sweat. My breathing has become shallower as the effort it takes to control the Revokers, especially in human form, starts making itself known.

"Are you ill?"

"It isn't easy controlling them," I admit. If I can't tell my clone, who can I tell?

Ryin's eyes immediately start to glow blue, causing me to jerk in surprise. He holds up his hands, appearing non-threatening, then hovers them over my head. A cool tingling sensation follows in their wake as he waves them back and forth. The pain and exhaustion fade away.

It's still there in the background, but retreats enough that I feel invigorated, like I've drunk some kind of magical energy juice. He really wasn't kidding about the healing thing. But now he's frowning.

"Victor," he says, saying my name like he's about to give me bad news.

"Yeah?"

"How long have you been ill?"

If he's some kind of magical healer, there's no use hiding the truth. Maybe he can even figure out some way to help. "It's come on slowly, over time. I was never meant to control the Revokers alone. When I got this ability, the daimon told me I needed my parallel in order to manage the Revokers once and for all."

"And did it tell you what would happen if you did not find your parallel?"

"You can give it to me straight, man. I'm dying, aren't I? At least that's what it feels like."

The glow retreats from his eyes, and he blinks as if it's difficult to see now without the power running through him. "I can do a little to help, but whatever is wrong with you is beyond my ability to heal permanently."

I blow out a breath—I hadn't really hoped for anything different. That would be too easy, and nothing about my life has ever been easy.

He drops his gaze. "You believe Celena is your parallel?"

Isn't that the question of the hour? "I thought so when we first met, but maybe it was just that I recognized her because I'd known Talia. Though I didn't really know her. She was a lot younger, and I wasn't allowed to mix with the family of my mom's boss. At any rate, I do feel something for Celena. But she would need a daimon for us to be sure, and trying for another one has an equal shot at killing her."

"And what happens to the Revokers if you die?" His expression is serious.

"Pretty sure they're waiting for that. It's what they want. I'm a problem for them. Listen, you have to figure out a way to evacuate the city. The ones down south, they're coming. I'm not connected to them; they're too far away for me to really sense them, but I just know. Eventually, they're going to make their way up here and there aren't enough of you to fight them off."

Ryin is about to say something but is interrupted by a commotion among the soldiers. He rises and I stand as well, though dizziness swamps me as I get to my feet and I have to reach out a hand to the wall to stay upright.

Wings flap overhead, and then an enormous golden eagle swoops down to the ground. Within a moment, it transforms into a brown-skinned guy with his black hair in a ponytail. A younger, pale-skinned man rushes through the crowd and greets him with a fist to his chest, then starts talking almost too fast to be understood.

"Sir Harshal, the Fai section of the wall is being hit. There are at least two dozen Revokers digging through. Fai soldiers are beating them back, but more Revokers keep arriving to replace those they drive away."

My stomach drops. It's already happening. The groups attacking now may be small, but with that unending supply of monsters to the south, it won't be long now. Is this some kind of strategy at play? I hadn't thought they were organized or intelligent enough for that, but what do I know?

All this effort at keeping a dozen of the creatures outside the wall here is just pressing pause on the inevitable. If there are other breaches, then everyone here will suffer. And I can't be in two places at once.

The guy with the ponytail appears to be in charge and barks out orders, sending troops down that way to support the Fai while instructing the people up here filling in the hole to work faster.

If things continue the way I think they will, there won't be much left for anyone to rule over, regardless of what happens to Celena.

TWENTY-TWO

Celena

SHAD OFFERS to find a place for me to stay in the city. Apparently, the majority of the buildings in our settlement are still intact and can house people—though few are currently set up as residences. However, many of the most high-ranking citizens are taking the units available instead of bedding down in the arena with the rabble. But I'd rather go back to Victor.

I'm beyond exhausted from the day's activities, and all I want is to see him again. Recalling how he looked when I left him, pale and sweating, as if the effort of maintaining his hold on the Revokers was draining, makes me want to ensure he's all right. My journal tells of bloody noses and seeing him collapsed on the floor. Part of me just wants to see him with my own eyes and not accept the word of people I'm still not sure I can trust.

Dominga makes her opinion on the matter clear. She thinks I should return to the heart of our territory and sleep in "a situation befitting my station." It sounds lovely, and if Victor could go too, I would. I still haven't had that hot bath I've been longing for.

When I inform her that I'm going back to the wall for the night, she turns away in a snit and stomps off. However, I have a feeling her annoyance won't last, or perhaps annoyance is her constant state of being, so this mood doesn't signify.

Shad assigns an honor guard of soldiers to accompany me back to the wall. I'm tense and keep my eye on them but am no longer truly worried about an assassination attempt.

The trip is quick, made in the dark with only the headlights of the vehicle cutting through the gloom. At night, this remnant of a city is spooky. Full of hollowed-out buildings, rusted husks of cars, and vegetation taking over everything unless it's been purposefully beaten back. This place does not feel like home to me, especially these abandoned sections.

A camp has sprung up along the base of the wall in my absence, and the signs of life are heartening. The evening has grown cool; fires dot the landscape, some in round metal trash bins, some inside of circles of rock and rubble on the ground. Repairs to the breach in the concrete are continuing through the night, and tents have been set up to accommodate all the soldiers here.

After climbing out of the vehicle, I spot Ryin and Talia seated at one of the fires. For a moment, my heart lurches, seeing the lean man in profile and thinking he's Victor, but flames illuminate a face free of scars.

The two men hold themselves differently as well. Ryin has the taut bearing of someone who's been trained with unyielding discipline, while Victor moves more languidly, his bones seeming to be made of something a little more flexible than the steel that runs through Ryin's spine.

Then Ryin drapes an arm casually around Talia's shoulders, pulling her closer in a move that sparks instant jealousy in me. She is out in the open with her parallel, her love. She has a dragon within her. It's hard not to feel animosity for the woman who shares my face and has the things I long for.

I nearly trip over the gravel. Yes, the dragon is something I've always wanted, but love? A full body shiver takes hold. I do not love Victor, that's ridiculous. I barely know him. True, he has my trust and my loyalty, but he has earned those in the brief acquaintance I can recall and even before, if my journal is to be believed. How can I love anyone when I barely know who I am?

Envying Talia is beneath me. She has only been kind and helpful; there's no cause for such feelings. Though watching her smile up at Ryin causes my heart to clench. Melancholy descends.

I draw closer to them, working to pull my expression into neutrality, hoping my distress does not show.

"He's just over there," Ryin says before I can even speak, pointing to a tent that looks lonely set up a little ways away from the others.

"Thank you."

Ryin looks like he wants to speak. He shares a glance with Talia, and my shoulders tense. "What is it?" I ask.

"Nothing. Or rather, nothing that is mine to say." His eyes are hooded, and his words bear secrets. "Have a good night, Your Grace."

Whatever he's hiding irritates me, but I'm far too weary to pursue it tonight. I nod at them in as regal a way as I can muster, then turn on my heel and march toward the tent he pointed out.

"Victor?" I call out, crouching at the entrance. I don't want to startle him; he might be asleep. But the flaps ripple open, and he pokes his head out.

"So you've survived?" His voice is dry, but it's the best thing I've heard in hours. And he looks better; he's not pouring sweat, and his coloring, as far as I can tell in the dim light, is healthy. He moves aside so I can crawl into the tent.

"How did it go?" he asks.

I settle onto the small nest of blankets inside. The thin material of our temporary dwelling holds in warmth, and it's almost cozy in here. These cannot be considered luxury accommodations, but there's no place I'd rather be.

I tell him how I spent my afternoon: meeting my people, being interrogated by the councilors. Overwhelmed with love and adoration on one hand and confronted with distrust on the other.

"It'll keep you humble," Victor says, his lips twisted in a half-smile.

"I don't know how I'm going to do this," I admit, allowing my shoulders to slump. The exhaustion of the day has definitely caught up with me, but the uncertainty won't let go either.

"Are you sure you even want to be queen? Seems like a lot of trouble and not much reward if the way Shad is living is any sign. I imagined you in a palace with servants and flutes of champagne floating through the air to your lips, not…" He waves an arm around. "A camp in the dirt at the edge of the apocalypse."

My lips curve as I consider his question, the same one I've been asking myself. Do I want to be queen?

I search the gaping chasm of my memory for any other purpose, any other goals. Of course, there are none. I have one path leading in a straight line from the knowledge within me, and it's honed and focused to a single point.

"They offered me a more permanent dwelling," I say. "But I wanted to be with you." He actually seems surprised.

"You're the only one I trust here," I whisper. The weight of everything I've been through over the past few days finally falls down on me. I don't want to cry, but tears stream down my cheeks without my permission.

Victor slides forward and wraps me in his arms, then pulls us down on the blankets. Inside the cradle of his strength, I'm warm and safe. Outside this flimsy tent lies an army with no loyalty to me, and on the other side of the wall we're against, vicious monsters are out for blood. But with Victor, all of that fades away. At least for a little while.

The overflowing gush of emotion within me ebbs away,

and I can appreciate the firm feeling of his chest beneath my cheek. "So, I can stay?"

He chuckles. "Of course, princess. How could I turn you away?"

I snuggle into him, my eyelids growing heavy. "You know the story of Adom and Evelyn?" I ask, fighting sleep.

"Hmm?"

"I wrote about it in my journal. Then I found the original in the library. It was handwritten in a blank book, isn't that strange?"

He squeezes me just a bit closer. "Yeah, I thought so too. The only story in there too, like whoever the author was had wanted to get it out and then had nothing else to say. What about it?"

"I was just thinking that it needs a happier ending. I don't like the way it ends."

"What do you want to have happen, then?"

I think about that for a few moments. "Evelyn comes back to meet Adom, the man she loves. It's on one of those days he'd wandered to the edge of the two lands just to be closer to her. He sees someone approaching from a distance and waits, discovering it's her."

My chest warms as I get on a roll. "Turns out there was a magical curse that prevented her from leaving to go back to him. If she steps one foot over the border, everything they sacrificed would be lost and the evil king would destroy the fragile peace she worked so hard to achieve. But she's never forgotten him.

"Neither of them can cross the border without terrible consequences. But they can embrace as long as they keep their feet in their respective lands. And that's what they do; they hold each other all night long until dawn breaks. In the light of day, they each know what they have to do. Their tasks are important, and it means they can't be together right then. But one day, they'll be together forever."

My tears are back by the time I finish. I don't know where the story came from. Is it something I do often, telling tales, or is it just this moment, this story that's touched my heart?

"That's still pretty sad," Victor whispers into my hair.

"Yes," I admit. "But not quite so sad."

His only response is to tighten his arms around me. And that's how I fall into a dreamless sleep.

TWENTY-THREE

Celena

BREAKFAST IS a lumpy orange mash that makes me long for the meals Victor prepared in his fortress. Those were crunchy and flavorful. I scoop this unappetizing slush and shovel it into my mouth, knowing it's providing nutrients I desperately need but not enjoying the taste one bit.

Victor finds this hilarious but refuses to tell me why. I suppose it has to do with something I did or said before I lost my memory, so I shrug it off. We eat seated around the remnants of a fire on the ground with half a dozen soldiers. The men and women eye him with wariness but are deferential likely because of how I treat him. I'm glad for it.

It's just as we're finishing that a brown bear runs down the street toward the camp with an easy gait. With a flash of light and the hint of sulfur, the bear transforms into Zanna.

"The librarian has found something, Your Grace," she announces without preamble.

It's early in the morning, and the camp bustles with activity. The construction work that has been going on all night is nearly wrapped up; the hole in the wall is almost completely patched. But dozens upon dozens of soldiers, both in human and shifted forms, still patrol the area on high alert.

"He's waiting for you," Zanna says. "We're fresh out of dampeners, so we found a private place for you two to talk."

I stand and brush off my pants, handing my plate to Victor. He rises as well and, while I can't read his expression, the pain is back in his eyes, the strain clear.

"How is it today?" I whisper, leaning toward him.

"I'm managing," he says tersely.

I address one of the soldiers who's completed her meal. "Find Ryin, ask him to come here." The young woman jumps up and jogs off. Then I turn to Zanna. "Let's go."

She motions me forward. I squeeze Victor's hand before letting it go to follow the soldier down the pockmarked street.

We end up four blocks away in front of a cement structure. This building doesn't appear to have been constructed with any windows and, aside from some cracks marring the surface, is intact. But while she moves to the entry, suspicion has me pausing.

When I don't follow her in, Zanna looks at me over her shoulder, raising a brow.

"Why are we so far away from the others?"

She turns to face me. "Some of those cats can hear a mouse's heartbeat from two hundred feet away. Do you want your conversation private or not, Your Grace?"

I don't appreciate her tone and am still not convinced this isn't some kind of trap. She blows out a loud breath at my wariness.

"If Shad had wanted to end your life, Princess, wouldn't he have done it on the way home last night when you were alone with guards he hand-selected? Or maybe he could have poisoned your breakfast or any of the meals you ate yesterday? Or had your throat slit during the night?"

I hold up a hand. "Point taken. But if you were in my position, would you trust easily?"

"I don't trust easily now," she murmurs.

I take another look at the building and our quiet, apparently empty surroundings before cautiously following her inside.

Akeem waits in a high-ceilinged interior space lit with several lanterns. This place looks to have once been a warehouse. The smell of burning oil permeates the air. He does his odd little bow with his trunk in the air before straightening. Zanna salutes, either me or him, I'm not sure, and then leaves.

"What did you learn?" I ask as soon as her footsteps retreat.

"A great deal, Your Grace. I saved my findings into the library's archive. You can access it using this." With his trunk, he picks up a slim device lying next to the closest lantern. It's some kind of data tablet. "I think it best you listen for yourself."

I reach for the gadget, which appears to be comprised of two thin clear sheets with blue liquid sloshing and moving inside of it. "How do I...?" Knowledge of how to use this device is not something I've retained.

"Tablet, replay the most recent entry," Akeem calls out.

In my hands, the device lights up, the liquid swirling and changing. A voice comes out of it—one identical to Akeem's.

"'Lost Ones' is a term used by daimon spirits to describe those among their number who have revoked the standard notion of a covenant and, instead of merely desiring to observe and experience the material world, seek to impact it.

"Whereas most daimons unite with a living host and offer their powers in exchange for the experience of mortality, Lost Ones choose to inhabit the corporeal forms of the dead. It is a practice looked down upon by the majority of daimon spirits."

Shock and revulsion flow through me as the voice continues.

"No covenant can be created with the dead, and as such, no rules are followed, which allows for the perpetuation and expansion of chaos. The goal of the Lost Ones is to turn all humans into what we term Revokers."

My hands shake. Suddenly the air in here feels thin.

"Historically, Lost Ones have been kept in check by volunteer Sentinel daimons whose purpose is not merely to observe and report but actively maintain balance in the material world. They are somewhat analogous to human law enforcement, though they do not mete out punishment as we understand it.

"Very few daimons volunteer for such duties, as it is far more unpleasant than the normal covenant agreements. Sentinels are also quite selective about the humans who host them and reject more than the typical daimon does. But those whom they choose receive unique abilities to aid in their Sentinel's tasks."

The voice ends, the recording apparently finished, and my heart sinks. "Did it say anything about my particular daimon?" I whisper.

"That is all the information I was able to glean." Akeem's real voice is different from the one coming out of the little tablet. Warmer and more compassionate.

Air saws in and out of my lungs; I think I might need to sit down. If my daimon is a Sentinel, it sounds like they're finicky about their hosts. And mine has already rejected me twice.

Did it think me unworthy? Then what was all that about being destined for a Sentinel? Becoming the queen who is needed to stop the Lost Ones? How can I do any of that if it doesn't choose me?

And Victor...I *must* be his parallel. His daimon must be a Sentinel as well, with unique abilities over the Lost Ones—the Revokers.

How can I convince my daimon that I am deserving of the task and the responsibility? That I can help Victor, somehow, and fight off the creatures who are determined to kill us all?

"Where are the bliss trials held?" I ask.

Akeem's eyes grow wide. "The levels of bliss in the city have been sabotaged to a critical extent. At the moment, the only sources large enough for complete submersion are the data storage bays in the library. But you understand the implications of the recording, right, Your Grace?"

I unclench my jaw long enough to answer. "I failed twice already, and this is the reason. I'm aware that a third failure will kill me, Akeem, but I can't sit back and do nothing. This is my purpose, and I have a duty to fulfill it. Besides, without a daimon, I am nothing. I don't belong here. I have no place." My voice wavers at the end as the grim reality settles into my bones.

"That is not necessarily the case, Your Grace. Your people love you. I heard of the welcome you received yesterday. Is that not proof of their regard?"

The question is kindly said but nevertheless pierces me. Is it enough to be alive and loved but useless, or should I risk everything for a chance to be more? To fulfill my destiny?

A vision of this morning comes into focus, clearing away the haze in my mind. Awaking in Victor's arms, warm and safe and feeling like I belonged there. In another world, perhaps the one he hails from, could that have been my life? I know deep down in my remaining soul that would be enough for me.

Even if we could have lived back in that tower in the city across the water, spending our days in the library, reading and re-reading all the books, painting murals, growing vegetables...I could have loved that life as well. Maybe we could have stayed like that forever.

The choices before me are dizzying. My daimon has deemed me unsuitable twice before, and I don't want to die.

If I never did the trial again, I could relearn all that I've lost with my memory soul. I could create some kind of life here, couldn't I?

But just as that thought settles, spreading a cozy warmth over my chest, Zanna rushes in. "We have to get you to safety. There's another breach in the wall."

TWENTY-FOUR

Victor

PAIN EXPLODES INSIDE MY HEAD, and a warm flow of blood streams down from my nose. The Revokers outside the wall burble with excitement and move off to the west at a rapid pace. Their departure should relieve the crushing weight pressing on me, but it does nothing.

I've been sitting most of the morning, back against the wall, as I did yesterday, focusing on keeping the monsters out. It's only when I try to stand that I realize the true toll holding them back has been taking on me. My legs buckle and nearly crumple under me, so I rest my shoulder against the wall, allowing it to hold me up.

A story my teacher once told comes to mind. It's about boiling a frog—starting in cold water and slowly heating it so it doesn't know it's being cooked...or something like that. That must be what happened to me. Controlling the Revokers initially wasn't drawing that much from me because of the boomerang effect thing, but over the past two days, it's drained practically everything I have.

Murmurs become shouts ringing out around me. My vision swims as I try to step away from the wall. Then Ryin is up in my face, eyes glowing blue, hands hovering on either side of my head. Each time he's healed me, it's helped less and less; this time, though the same cool sizzle vibrates across my skin, I barely feel any difference.

"They're leaving," I croak out. "Joining others to the west." I'm sure about this, even though the others are too far away for me to feel. But there was joy and anticipation in the emotions of those who just left.

Something is happening that made them excited. Something I can't stop. Something I'm far too weak to do anything about at all.

Even though the wall is holding me up, it's still not enough. My legs give out completely; I slide down in a heap.

Ryin calls my name. I flutter my eyes open, but they weigh about five hundred pounds now. Blood spills out of my nose and ears. From the corner of my eye, I see it pooling on the gravel-covered ground.

I open my lips, wanting to speak, to get a message to Celena—tell her I'm sorry. But the words won't come out. And then I can no longer keep my eyes open and there's only darkness.

AT FIRST, I think I'm in the Origin again, the place these people believe you go when you die. But instead of being surrounded by a white, all-encompassing light, I can't see anything. Maybe my eyes are still closed, but I think it's just black here.

I try to move and gravel shifts under my hip. So I'm not quite dead yet, but I'm not sure I'm entirely alive.

Here in this in-between place, I sense them all. The Revokers. Closer than ever.

The writhing mass I saw the other day gathering to the south—they're on the move. On the way. Others sent ahead have already breached the wall in two places west of here and are pouring into the city right now.

This is the endgame.

For some reason, my connection to them is stronger than it's ever been. I sense with utter clarity something I've never understood before: what these creatures are after.

It's like I've joined their collective hive mind, and part of the orientation includes a history lesson. Images interrupt the endless field of black that is my vision. There's my city, Oakland, whole and intact in the world before the Sorrows, only it's not the version I knew back home. The Trib tower, where I've lived for the past twelve years, glints in the sunlight, a neon sign spelling out "OHLONE" on all four sides of the tower. At least I finally have the answer to that mystery.

Even though it's not quite my Oakland, everything seems to look and function in basically the same way. People hurry to work, honk their car horns, wait impatiently in line at coffee shops.

Then the images move into fast forward, a montage of clips that I have to focus on in order to follow.

A crowd of angry protesters turns into a mob. People race through the streets throwing rocks, looting, dragging people from cars. Images of turmoil, tragedy, disease, poverty, destruction, misery, and death flit by.

Natural disasters strike, leaving a trail of wreckage in their wake. The earth convulses violently, its tremors toppling entire cities. Torrential storms unleash with fury. Seas rise, ice caps melt, whole species of animals are destroyed in what seems like the blink of an eye. Fear hangs like smoke in the air, as citizens frantically search for shelter amid the chaos. The sky becomes a battlefield. Bombs plummet from above, raining down hell upon the terrified populace. It's a horrifying spectacle, playing out like some nightmarish B-movie.

And then it's over. Along with most of humanity. But the shifters' numbers are barely impacted. After generations of hiding from humans, staying to themselves in concealed enclaves, they managed to make it out of the apocalypse relatively unscathed. Afterwards, both clans, the Fai with their glowing eyes and the Nimali who change forms in the blink of an eye, seek new homes out of the remains of the destruction.

The Fai use their gifts to grow forests in places where the bliss bubbles out of the earth. There, they make their communities. Keeping to their woodland homes, they honor the bliss, hold it sacred, and use it to inspire them.

Nimali apply their ingenuity to experimenting with the bliss they mine—transforming it, creating new technology and innovations. Eventually, their entire society relies upon bliss, and they don't remember how life worked without it.

And since bliss is so essential to the life and culture of both clans and is a limited resource, they fight over it. Bloody battles have been waged for generations over a single bliss matrix. In this city, where the matrices were once so plentiful, the war has been especially brutal. The Fai believe they are protecting it, while the Nimali believe it is their right to use it.

Both clans require the substance to unite with their daimons. They submerge their young adults in the liquid and celebrate when the men and women emerge with hitchhiker spirits riding within their bodies, spirits who learn, watch, grow, and experience mortality in a way they could never do in the Origin.

I see it from the perspective of the Revokers, the spirits who refuse to sublimate their will to those of humans. Who aren't content to be passengers sharing power and allowing humans to make all the decisions.

They've seen what happens when people with power use it poorly and are not convinced the covenants the clans strike will hold.

So they do some innovation of their own and find a way to use the dead instead of the living to experience the world.

They transform discarded bodies into twisted creatures, red-eyed, poison-clawed, with one goal: to end it all.

But to do that, the Revokers need to convert everyone, transform every person alive into one of them, and then it will all stop. The horror, the cruelty, the fighting, the death, the war. All of it, over.

Revokers believe the only way to get the two clans to stop fighting each other over the bliss they both use and cherish is if none are left to fight at all.

They show me these things as if to say, "You are stopping us from our higher mission. All we want to do is end the suffering." It's a twisted way to find peace, but that's what they're after. Real supervillain-type stuff.

Of course, they don't see themselves that way; they feel like they're saving their siblings—the ones locked into covenants that will ultimately fail because of the frailty of people.

Whatever it is that prevents them from going underground or over water—some limitation baked into the way they take over dead bodies instead of uniting with living ones—has kept them from tunneling through the wall for decades. Ironically enough, it was the former king's cruelty, Celena's father's capture and experimentation on them, that gave them the means to overcome the eight-foot-thick obstacle keeping them from their goal.

They show me things I don't understand. Bliss and another substance that's its antithesis. How they harnessed that other substance to get access to this world. How the nightmarish experiments the old king carried out were communicated back to the hive mind and let them know how much those bodies could withstand.

Digging through the wall is painful for them, torturous even. The cement contains iron and salts that burn them. But by spreading the pain out among the group, taking turns and then retreating to heal, they can continue endlessly.

The images playing in front of me stop, but the emotions continue. The Revokers are close. So close to their goal. Excitement fills them.

My abilities to control them have been just a speed bump on their road to the total annihilation of all human life in this place. And now that I'm nearly spent, I won't be around to annoy them much longer.

All my senses start to fade. Even the feeling of the rocks beneath me is no longer a sharp pain. I'm reaching the end of my endurance. But then they send me one last message, which practically stops my heart cold.

They show me the only way to stop them.

Maybe they share it because they know I can't do anything with the information, or because if I had ever found my parallel, we would have still needed to do this and would never have succeeded.

Either way, the knowledge comes too late. My body fails and I'm locked not just in darkness but emptiness, wishing I could have done more.

TWENTY-FIVE

Celena

THE CAMP IS in chaos when we return. Shad and his other military advisors are there, everyone facing different directions and barking out orders as people transform into predator animals before racing or flying away.

I spin around in a circle amid the madness, unsure of my place in all of this. I can't help. Can't shift. Don't know how to command an army.

Then I spot Ryin and the crumpled heap he's crouched over. The Fai man's eyes glow blue and his movements are desperate, hands jerking as they hover over Victor's face and chest.

Victor. Who isn't moving at all.

Talia appears out of nowhere, arriving at Ryin's side at the same time as I do. I crash onto the ground, skinning my knees, to cradle Victor's head in my hands.

"What happened?"

Ryin's voice cracks. "He's dying."

"*Dying?* Why?"

"There's no physical cause that I can heal. His life force, it's just draining away."

"I don't understand. How is this happening? He's not even controlling the Revokers anymore."

"I'm not certain, but I think…" He trails off, brow crinkling.

"What?" I ask, trying to control the frenzy clawing at me.

"I think it's his daimon."

"A daimon can't kill its host, can it? Is this something I've forgotten?"

"I don't get the sense that it's *trying* to kill him, but something else is at play." He looks at Talia uncertainly. "I wonder if it's because he's not from here. Maybe the daimons interact with people from your world differently?"

"But my daimon brought me to this world because of you," she says, "because you're its parallel. I can only imagine he was brought here for a similar reason."

Understanding crashes into me, stealing my breath. He won't survive without his parallel. I lay his head down gently, glad to see that his chest still rises and falls, albeit worryingly slow.

"Can you keep him breathing?" I ask Ryin.

"I'll do my best," he replies. "But I'm not sure for how long."

I rise, determination hardening. Just beyond the little bubble where Victor lies dying, an ordered chaos prevails as the Nimali urgently prepare for an attack. Somewhere in the city not far from here, Revokers are pouring in and rampaging. But I can't do anything about that. Not yet.

"I need to do the trial." I say it aloud to no one in particular, then spot Akeem standing a few paces away.

I march up to him. "Can I do the trial in the library?"

"It's been done before." He looks at Talia, who has followed me over.

"Dominga said you left to find an untouched pool of bliss to use," Talia says quietly behind me.

I spin around to face her. "Yes, and it didn't seem to help

at all, so I'll take any I can get at this point. I can't just sit around and do nothing. I'll beg my daimon if that's what it takes."

Her lips purse in thought. Then her gaze skates back to where the man she loves hovers over the man I...over Victor, still alive, but for how long?

"I know a place where you can do the trial." Her voice is low, pitched for my ears. "A pool of bliss where no trials have ever been done. It's as pure as it gets."

"Why would you help me?" I ask. I no longer have time for suspicion; I'm honestly just curious.

"Let's just say you remind me of someone," she says with a sad grin. "And if that man lying over there was brought to this world for you, I think we all need to find out."

SINCE EMERGING from the bliss pool with nothing but the desire to become a dragon blazing in my mind, I've considered many times what it would be like to be one. Never have I thought about what it would be like to ride on one. But Talia says the best way to get there is to fly, then leads me away from the fray and shifts into her green dragon form. She is considerably smaller than Shad's blue dragon, but still large enough to be formidable.

She hunkers down and allows me to climb on her shoulders. I grip the thorny edges protruding from her neck and hold on for dear life as her wings flap and we rise into the air.

My stomach swoops as we head north and west. I want to look over my shoulder to see if I can make out any of the destruction happening at the new breach in the wall, but I'm afraid if I turn, I'll fall. According to Zanna, both Fai and Nimali forces are uniting to beat back the tide of Revokers swarming through. How many will lose their lives?

But the only thing I can do is continue on the path I've set.

It may take a miracle for me to succeed, but it's the only option I have left.

We soar over the desiccated remains of the city, our path leading us toward an unending forest of vibrant green that engulfs nearly half of this peninsula. The sight is breathtaking in the soft, golden glow of the early afternoon sun, but melancholy washes over me as the ominous clouds approach, shrouding this beauty in darkness. I curl in on myself, a shiver coursing through me, the biting cold at this altitude gnawing at my very core.

We pass no visible buildings—it's just trees all the way to the ocean. The atmosphere of the Fai lands is peaceful, a respite from the forlorn destruction of the largely empty city. A green, lush retreat so different from the concrete and cement that I've seen since arriving.

As my vision fills with the quiet greenery around us, my thoughts are all on one question: How can I persuade my daimon to unite with me?

Talia lands in a small clearing where I less than gracefully slide off her back. Then she shifts and leads me to a set of stone steps disappearing underground.

"Will you be in trouble for bringing me here?" I ask as we descend, my voice hushed.

"The Fai are already suspicious of me because I change forms, though I'm not Nimali. It's just how my daimon chose to express itself. But I'm pretty sure they've got bigger fish to fry right about now." The way she speaks, her strange turns of phrase, reminds me of Victor, and a pang shoots through me.

Then we emerge in an underground oasis and I get my first look at the bliss pool. Though it's half the size of the pool I woke up beside, the one I'd done my last trial in, it's far more serene and plenty large enough for what I need.

There are alcoves and side caves, which Talia checks to ensure we're alone. "It's clear," she announces.

I swallow, fear and determination rising within me. I take a deep breath and step to the edge.

"If I don't make it back, please tell Victor that I'll see him in the Origin."

Before Talia can respond, I slip into the pool.

TWENTY-SIX

Celena

As soon as I open my eyes, my memories rush back in a torrential wave. Each moment, every hope and every dream from my entire life, surges through me. From childhood adventures to teenage humiliations to the heartbreak of losing the woman who meant everything to me.

My mother's gentle smile flashes before me, though I also recall how the light in her eyes dimmed each year. The warmth of my father's loving embrace wraps around me, even as the calculations in his stare chill me to the bone.

The weight of the memories of my past failures crashes down as well. My plans to leave and leash a daimon. My confidence and arrogance. And the endless days lost in the darkness of the tunnels, hope fading as hunger gripped me ruthlessly.

And Victor—stranger, savior, jailer. His wry tone and haunted gaze skating over my skin. His heated expression, the feel of his lips on mine. Everything I felt for him before, mixed with what I feel for him now. He was entirely unexpected. The ache that spreads from my bones to my head to my heart feels far too much like love.

The jarring sensation of having my life and memories

back begins to fade, and the Origin spreads out around me, a field of pristine white. Here, I exist as a disembodied spirit, suspended in this ethereal realm.

"Hello?" I call out with my mental voice, hoping upon hope that there is someone here to greet me.

"Celena." That is not the non-human communication of a daimon spirit. The all-too-familiar smiling tone fills me with joy, comfort, and incredulity.

"Mother?"

And then she's here. Not visible because this is not a place of vision, but the sense of her, the feel of her, the energy of her surrounds me like a thick blanket. Like the last hug she gave me before she was gone.

"How...What...? I don't understand. How are you here?" Even my mental voice stutters in shock. The Origin is a place of spirit, yes, but to actually talk to someone you knew after they'd gone...I've never heard of such.

"Celena, my darling. I can hold you here for a little while, but we don't have much time. The recordings I left for you were sadly incomplete. There is one truth I could never bring myself to share, not until it was too late. And I'm afraid it has left you unprepared for the task ahead of you."

To be in the presence of my mother again is indescribably beautiful. And heartbreaking. Emotions wash over me so powerfully they're difficult to withstand. I wish I could see her, touch her, hug her. How long have I yearned to be able to speak to her just one more time?

"It was my destiny to become the queen who was needed and stop the Revokers' scourge," she says. "But I failed. And though it is not fair to ask you to do what I could not, that is what is necessary, my dear. The cost of doing what must be done was more than I could bear, and to burden you with it... it's unconscionable. And I am sorry."

I don't understand. I'm trying to, but between the shock

of her presence here and her confusing words, I feel like I'm being battered about by vicious winds in a terrible storm.

"You are strong, my daughter. You have the will to do what I could not. I know you will not make the same mistakes that I did."

"What mistakes?"

But before she can answer, another presence arrives. This one is the polar opposite of my sweet and gentle mother and turns the storm into a tempest strong enough to rip limbs away from bodies.

"Celena, my girl," the rich voice booms in my head.

"Father?" My thoughts have completely stopped, stunned into a silence quieter than death.

"You are so bright and beautiful, even here."

I've scarcely had time to come to grips with his death, haven't had a breath to grieve, and now he's here. "I don't understand how either of you are able to be here speaking with me?"

"The daimons have allowed it," he says. "This is a critical time. Much depends on your decision today. You have been granted an opportunity very few have ever experienced."

"What is that?" I ask, working to get my mind back online and functioning.

"A choice," my father replies. "Two daimons await your decision."

"*Two* daimons? How is that even possible?"

"My darling daughter, you have made it possible. The strength of will I always knew you possessed has aligned with the dire situation faced by our people." His praise puffs me up as it always has. Part of me cringes at this.

"A dragon daimon awaits to be leashed by you," he continues. "One that would allow you to challenge and defeat the usurper currently occupying my throne. This dragon has a strength the likes of which has not been seen in generations. Your rule will be long and your name cherished by the Nimali for eternity." His deep voice resonates with pride.

Though I'm already weightless, a lightness fills me, making me feel extra floaty. Everything I dreamed of within my grasp.

"Your other option," my mother says, "is the daimon you were *meant* to have. Victor's parallel."

The bright bubble of my joy crashes to the ground with a pop. "They're not one and the same?"

"No, my dear, they're not. If you choose the daimon I intended for you, the one you have rejected twice before, then you can both save the man you love and destroy the Revokers forever."

I'm too stunned for a moment to respond. Finally, I'm able to form a coherent thought. "But I didn't reject anything."

"You arrived demanding a dragon, darling. Sentinel daimons are choosier than most and easily offended. You rejected it before even hearing its offer."

Guilt rattles through me like a thunderclap. She's right. I *had* come here making immediate demands. The daimon I met in my last trial was testy and rightfully so. This mess is entirely of my own making.

"And this Sentinel, the one you want me to choose, it is not a dragon?"

My father's voice booms. "Inferior is what it is. I beat back the Revokers for years with a dragon and Celena will do the same. Anything less would be an insult to our family line."

My mother, patient as she always was, ignores her husband and replies to me. "You could beat them back again and again, living in fear, while precious lives hang in the balance or, with the Sentinel, you can destroy the Revokers once and for all."

"At a cost too high to be borne," my father scoffs coldly.

"What is the cost?" My mental voice is meek, revealing my fear.

"It is the only way to save his life," my mother says. "And

the lives of everyone in the city. Does the cost still matter to you?"

Victor. How does my mother know what I feel before I even know? Before I even admit it to myself?

The choice laid out before me could not be more formidable. On one hand, everything I ever wanted, on the other, the man who means everything to me, and a permanent solution.

"Before I tell you what it will take, there is something else you should know," my mother admits, pain and regret clear in her tone. And then she tells me her story.

TWENTY-SEVEN

Victor

_____

A PRICKLY, tickling sensation like ants crawling over my skin draws me back from the deepest part of the darkness. It's an annoyance, an itch I can't scratch because I can't move my body.

Snatches of a voice whisper in my ear, but I can't grab hold of it at first. I think it sounds like my mother's.

I struggle to focus until it comes in more clearly. Then I'm sure of it. Ma is talking to me, asking me why I'm being so lazy, lying there on the dirty ground.

"Don't you have something you need to be doing, boy?" she says in a tone that's both playful but hints that if I don't find something to do, she will certainly find something for me.

I imagine her face, dark eyes flashing, mouth quirked like she's about to smile, though she rarely did. That vision or memory is something for me to hold on to, and I clutch it with a grip stronger than iron. Slowly, the fog covering my brain clears, and I wrest enough control over my body to open my eyes.

Just as Ma said, I'm lying on the dirty ground, rocks poking my back and hips. The only things in my field of vision are the wall rising over me and Ryin on the ground beside me. He looks up, eyes widening when I groan and shift.

"They're coming." My voice is half gravel, half frog. Inside that sense that connects me to the Revokers, I feel the approach of thousands like a relentless drumbeat. It accompanies their steps like a death march, and I can't escape it.

I wrestle my body into a seated position, pulling at whatever's left of my strength in order to do so.

"They're here," Ryin says. "They've breached the wall in two places to the west."

Terror seizes me. But somehow, I'm still alive. I don't know if I can do anything to stop this invasion, but I have to try. Which means I have to stand.

Once he figures out what I'm trying to do, Ryin helps me up. He keeps talking, but every last drop of energy in my body is going into holding me upright, so his speech sounds as if he's underwater.

Something must be going on with my brain, but I don't stop to think about it—I just will my legs into motion. Whatever gas I have left in the tank has to go toward getting to the breaches and doing whatever I can. Maybe buy enough time for more people to evacuate.

"Don't stand too close," I say, or think I say, but my own words feel like jelly in my mouth now. I stumble a few steps away, dig deep within to find the monster, and call it forward.

A pop of light, a whiff of sulfur, and the transformation is complete. Thick scaly hide. Giant bony wings. Razor-tipped claws. I blink my eyes, knowing they must be red, though I've never seen them. I'm bigger than any Revoker I've ever encountered, but maybe that's why I can control them.

All sound around us in the camp dies, as everyone gets a glimpse of what I really am. Who they've been harboring. Hopefully, they understand by now that I'm on their side. I may look like one of the enemy, but I'm not. However, inside my head, the creatures are louder than ever. Their desire to get through the wall screams at a fever pitch because they're actually doing it.

I spread my enormous wings and pulse them once, twice, then rise shakily into the sky. I'm a bit weak, but in this form, all my aches and pains fade away. Somehow my daimon is feeding me energy. I only hope that between the two of us, we have the strength to make some kind of difference here. Then at least I can die knowing I did everything I could.

I follow the wall toward the ocean. It's only a few minutes before I come to the battle. The breaches allowing the Revokers to plunge into the city are pretty close to one another, and half a dozen clusters of monsters are furiously digging to create more.

Nimali and Fai forces have combined to beat back the creatures as they enter, and the only thing that's saved the city so far is the funnel the breaches create. Only one of the Revokers can get through the hole at a time, and they are met with fierce opposition. But based on what I witness on the other side of the wall, this battle is hopeless.

The cats and bears and wolves and other animals, the birds of prey swooping down to attack, the—is that an abominable snowman? Some kind of Bigfoot-looking ice creature with white fur is holding its own against two red-eyed kaiju. Looks like the stuff of nightmares, but at least that thing's on our side. Then there are all the Fai, who appear human but effectively use their hands as claws, their teeth as fangs, and fly without wings to meet the enemy with vicious calculation.

It's like I've stepped right into the middle of a live action video game, but I have no time for wonder and awe. Because a swarm of Revokers like nothing I could have imagined is swiftly eating up the distance, racing across the barren wasteland to the south of the wall. I can't see them yet, but I feel them as they get closer and closer.

Those already here, the ones trying to get through the breaches, or digging additional tunnels, remind me of fast zombies in a movie. If they think about it hard enough, they might realize they could climb over one another to get on top of the wall. I hope this connection between us only goes one way—I don't want to give them any ideas.

My short flight has improved my energy a lot, oddly enough. I open my mouth and let out a roar, which echoes off the cement and broken asphalt. Avoiding all the other flying people and creatures, I dive on the outside of the wall and skim over the heads of the monsters.

I focus my energy and my intention and send them a single command. *LEAVE.*

My mental voice doesn't shout. I say it calmly and sternly, the way my old middle school principal used to talk. He got respect from the kids without ever raising his voice because when he said something, we all knew he meant it.

My order meets resistance. Like I thought, there are too many of them for me to control, but the dozen or so clambering to get through the two holes in the wall look up, their red glares cutting through the light mist that covers everything.

LEAVE. I repeat the command and feel an odd clicking in my chest that I've never experienced before. I'm not sure what it means. Is it my heart starting to fail? Though I'm not in any pain at the moment—thanks to the adrenaline, most likely— I'm at the end of my endurance.

But I fight with everything I've got; I can't die yet, dammit. I focus on giving the command several more times, but the clicking in my chest becomes insistent. It's like a time bomb waiting to go off. I open my mouth to bellow again, in anger and frustration, only instead of sound, a blaze of fire shoots out of me.

The flames hit a cluster of Revokers. They scream and shrink away, their hides smoking.

What is this new ability? I have no idea where it came from, but it's scaring them and stopping the relentless stream of monsters breaking through into the city. It's giving our soldiers on the other side a few more moments to mount their defense, so I decide to embrace it.

The question is, can I control it? I do another flyby over the heads of the kaiju, hoping to both keep more from entering and to stop the diggers from making any progress. They are really close to completing their goal and opening more breaches.

Once again, I unhinge my jaw and breathe fire.

It's easy enough to do and seems to come on demand. Now, I sweep back and forth, breathing fire straight down onto the Revokers with each pass.

In my peripheral vision, other winged creatures keep their distance, but a giant blue dragon approaches. The king is larger than me, and his thunderous war cry shakes the earth. I think he's gearing up for another yell, but this time when he opens his mouth, fire shoots out as well.

Of course, I know dragons breathe fire, but seeing it in real life and on the heels of my own discovery, it's jarring.

Just then, a group of Revokers evidently put their brains together, because one climbs on another's shoulders to reach out and grab hold of my foot. I've been staying low, to do as much damage as possible, but it put me too close to them.

Let go! My mental command works immediately on a single creature and it releases me, but not before scoring my ankle with its claws. I shoot a stream of flame toward it, my whole foot burning with poison.

In order to eject the toxin out of my body, I need to focus. Fortunately, it looks like Shad's fire is doing a good job of beating back the first wave of attackers. Though I'm constantly aware of the massive horde that's getting closer with each passing second.

My injury drains the newfound stamina I'd managed to find. The shift takes me over involuntarily—to my knowledge, I've never passed out in my Revoker form. I barely make it over the wall and haven't even landed before I'm human again and falling.

I land in a heap on my side. Several bones feel like they're crushed, but that pain can't compare to the blaze igniting my foot. Straining, I push all my mental control into the poison to force it from my body. Blood streams from my nose. My head swims.

Through bleary eyes, I see Ryin darting through the air toward me. I didn't realize he could fly—I really need to ask what his daimon is.

"I thought you said you were a Revoker," he says once he lands, peering at me as though he can see inside me.

"I am," I grind out.

"No, you're a dragon."

That's when I pass out.

TWENTY-EIGHT

Celena

WHEN I CLIMB out of the bliss pool, Talia is not there to greet me. The underground cave is quiet and deserted. It's just as well; I'd prefer to be alone with my thoughts right now.

The story my mother relayed causes chills to race up and down my spine, though this cavern is almost uncomfortably warm. Her lingering sorrow is a weight on my chest, threatening to demolish my heart.

With leaden legs, I climb the steps to the surface and stand for a moment under the canopy of trees. This forest is perfect in its serenity. However, the external vision of peace is at odds with the terrible storm raging inside of me, the result of the choice I never dreamed I'd be called upon to make.

But it's done now. My daimon chosen. The only thing left for me to do is shift.

The spirit now sharing my body is pleased to express itself. Even without me changing forms, it looks through my eyes, feels every sense that I have—the filtered light on my face, the crispness of the breeze against my skin, the faint smell of smoke in the air, the sound of distant screaming.

Urgency grips me. There will be plenty of time later to

adjust to the newness of knowing a spirit piggybacks my every move.

This clearing is wide enough to accommodate me, so I let the change take me. Closing my eyes against the bright flash of light that erupts from within, I breathe through the odd sensation of transformation.

When I open my eyes again, my vision is changed. I have an eye on each side of my head instead of both in the front, and my depth, distance, and light perception will take some getting used to.

I blink against the relative brightness of the overcast sky and unfurl the wings tucked against my sides. Having extra appendages is such an unusual feeling.

There's no time to delay, so I beat my wings and rise into the air. Fortunately, flying comes as naturally as breathing. My daimon's satisfaction is clear; it wants nothing more than to do what it came here for. I take a moment to get my bearings, then head for the wall.

Long before I arrive, the evidence of the conflict is clear. The scent of blood coats my nose. Nimali and Fai are in the fight of their lives. I discover where Talia has gotten to when a green dragon darts down from the clouds. She's joined by Shad's blue dragon, and together, they offer the first line of defense. Flying back and forth, they vent red, orange, and white arcs of fire onto the screaming mass of monstrous, red-eyed bodies.

At first, no one notices me, intent as they are all on their battles or tending the wounded. I'm just another creature in the sky amid flying Fai, birds of prey, and the few phoenixes and gryphons among the Nimali.

At the moment, the fighting is contained, but a sense of dread squeezes me, stealing my breath. It comes from deep within, a drumbeat of wrongness thudding louder and louder, getting closer and closer.

My keen vision zeroes in on a prone form on the ground:

Victor. He lies sprawled off to the side with enough space for me to land next to him, and I set down there. My four feet hit the ground and I retract my wings to my sides, sniffing at him with my newly sensitive nose.

I nudge at his forehead with my muzzle, concern rising. He's immobile as a corpse. Is his chest even rising and falling?

Then his eyes flutter open. A riot of relief lathers within me. At first, his gaze is unfocused, but the moment his vision sharpens, I hold my breath.

When he gets a good look at me, recognition sets in, and his lips part in shock. "Celena?" His voice is a mere whisper. "What are you?"

I cannot answer in this form, but my thoughts coalesce. I am the queen who is needed. At least, I hope so.

TWENTY-NINE

Victor

THE ONLY WORD for Celena's daimon form is magnificent. Her multicolored tail in shades of pink, purple, red, blue, and green whips gently back and forth. I take in her feathered wings, her elongated head and snout, and the gleaming, iridescent horn in the center of her head.

"You're a unicorn?" I whisper. "With wings?"

A voice to my left calls out in awe. "She's an alicorn." It's Talia. She approaches, looking weary, and clings to Ryin's side like a burr.

I've never heard of an alicorn before, but it seems to fit. And then Shad is there as well, stepping up closer to Celena. Her body is pure midnight black, the only color on her coming from her mane and tail, which both contain a rainbow's worth. Her horn shimmers with light and looks both magical and regal.

"There's never been..." Shad starts. "She's the first alicorn I've ever heard of."

She's brilliant. Beautiful. A tremor runs through me as the daimon within reacts to her presence as well.

Mine, it says.

A link locks into place between us. The alicorn's dark eyes

glint with Celena's challenge. It's her in there all right, so easy to recognize, like a neon sign screaming at me.

She takes a few steps back, flaps her wings, and gracefully takes to the sky, moving swiftly.

My daimon gives me a moment's warning. Earlier, I was sure I was on death's door, but right this second, I've never felt more alive. I jump to my feet, alarming the others, and jog away to find enough space to shift. Then I give over to the animal inside.

If Ryin is right and I really am a dragon and not a Revoker, as I've always thought, then I don't need to be concerned about others being afraid of me. My black scales glimmer as the sun peeks out from behind the clouds and I chase after Celena.

Down below, the base of the wall is clear of Revokers. Shad and Talia must have successfully wiped out this wave of attackers. I reach out my senses for the swarm that's on its way, but they've halted their forward progress. All that excitement and giddiness have fled. Caution dominates their energy now. Having their asses kicked might do that. Or maybe it's us.

I know this isn't over by a long shot, but it looks like we have a reprieve. Relief makes me unclench so much that I dip several feet in the sky. With a few flaps of my wings, I rise again and come parallel with Celena. She zips through the air in a playful way, and I pursue her. Excitement and energy run through my bloodstream as we fly.

I'm not sure how long we're up there for, but when we land, it's in a familiar place. She's taken us back to the gas station in the South Bay, close to the water, where we spent the night on our journey to the city.

We both settle on the ground in front of the dilapidated building. Celena shifts back to human first, and I follow.

She grins up at me, eyes shining and full of light and...

something else. Something I'm not sure I can think about too carefully.

She must have her memory back now with her daimon. That's how it works, right? So she remembers how we first met and what I did. But it doesn't look like she's holding a grudge. In fact, she steps closer to me and grabs both my hands in hers.

"When I was in the Origin," she says, her voice trembling, "I had to make a choice. It was between what I'd always thought I wanted and what I want now."

"I don't understand. What do you mean?"

She steps even closer until our toes are touching. A shiver races through me. "It doesn't matter. I chose you."

I blink, letting the weight of her words settle on my shoulders. The air around us thins as my heart speeds. "We're parallels. You feel it, right?"

She nods, appearing cautious. "I do."

"And…you're okay with that?" She knows what it means more than I do. Uncertainty and vulnerability have my stomach twitching.

But a smile spreads across her face, wide as the sea. "More than okay."

Then she kisses me. A rush of warmth spreads through my body. Her lips are softer than cotton, and she tastes sweet, like a melon. Every one of my nerve endings is electrified. I wrap my arms around her and pull her close to me until we're pressed together, no daylight between us.

I'm lost in her. My hands cup the sides of her face, trying to get her even closer. I'd pull her inside of me if I could.

She nips at my bottom lip, exploring and tasting. Holding her feels more right than anything ever has before. After minutes or hours of standing there on the crumbling street, she pulls away and rests her forehead on my chest, catching her breath.

"I brought us here because there's something you need to see," she says.

"Here?"

"Yes." She pulls back and takes my hand, leading me into the dark and rancid space where we crashed for the night. How long ago was that? Just a day or two, right? Feels like an eternity has passed since then.

"When I was in the Origin, I spoke to my parents. My mother revealed something she'd kept from me. I think…I think she was ashamed of it."

We walk through the shop area where we'd bedded down. Celena heads straight for a toppled metal shelf, one I hadn't bothered to investigate the first time we were here. She bends and looks like she's going to lift it, but it's way too heavy. When I move to help her, she just smiles and pulls it up with one hand. It swings back easily—the whole thing was hiding a concealed door.

The entry is low enough that I have to duck through, just an opening roughly carved into the wall. Beyond is a small room in far better shape than the space we just came from.

Cinderblock walls are all intact, one has a long crack that's been patched. A cot sits along one wall, neatly made up with sheets and a blanket, though everything is coated with a layer of dust. There are shelves of supplies, canned food, glass jugs of water. A lantern. First aid kit. Stack of books.

"Someone used to live here?" I say.

"If not live, then visit regularly," she replies.

I take in the neatly organized supplies, but Celena's attention is focused on an area on the wall. Light comes in from the doorway, but it's still pretty dark in here. I light the lantern, which still has fuel in it, and brighten the space.

Turns out she's standing in front of a sketch drawn right onto the cinderblocks with something like charcoal. It's a tough medium, almost impossible to get the lines right, but the artist, whoever they were, did a great job.

A man and a woman stand on either side of a barbed wire fence. Though the sketch is relatively simple, the expressions of longing on each of their faces are not.

Below each figure is a name. I suck in a breath when I read them. "Adom and Evelyn." I turn to Celena. "The story?"

Sorrow fills her eyes. "My mother's best friend since childhood was a boy named Amadi. As they grew up, they became more than friends. They were in love and planned to marry. But my mother's parents were powerful Cardinals, high-ranking aristocrats in our society. They didn't approve of him since he came from an Umber family. And there was a lot of pressure on Mother to leash a powerful daimon. She failed twice, just as I did. And if Amadi leashed a predator, he'd be more acceptable to her parents, so the two of them decided to follow the legends her grandmother told her and head across the water to find an untouched pool of bliss."

"That's how you learned about it?" I ask.

She nods. "They found the pool and did their trials and were both awarded very powerful daimons, Sentinel daimons, which allowed both of them to control the Revokers. And they were parallels."

Her eyes began to mist with tears, though the corners of her lips turn up slightly. "My mother was a dragon, a black dragon, and Amadi was an alicorn. Not a predator. But with her daimon, she knew she could go back to the Nimali and challenge King Lyon, my father's father, for the throne. As queen, she wanted to bring peace and prosperity to our people. And no one would question a queen's choice of consort. But in her absence, Lyon's son Lyall had also leashed a dragon."

Celena drops her head to my shoulder. I pull her into me as she continues. "They were headed back to the city, when they discovered a group of humans being attacked by Revokers. Amadi told her to go ahead while he stayed to help. He ended up escorting the group east and protecting them the entire way.

"My mother returned home to find a new dragon king on the throne, one larger and crueler than she was, and had a choice to make. Lyall offered her marriage—he envisioned an entire dynasty of dragons. Mother's Sentinel daimon believed that the best way to protect the Nimali was to accept his proposal. She could not have stayed married to him if her daimon had not agreed to the match. She felt she could temper my father's excesses and cruelties, and I think, to some extent, she did. But it meant that she could never be with the man she loved, never be with her true parallel."

Her shoulders shake as soft sobs rack her. I pull her even closer, wrapping both arms around her. With tears in her voice, she continues.

"Once Amadi discovered her marriage, he couldn't bear to live in the city and watch her with another man, so he stayed in the east, doing what he could to protect the migrating humans from the Revokers. But he would allow himself to come here to this place halfway between their homes to be closer to her. It was far enough that my father never caught on to his presence."

She points at the image on the wall, the names beneath the two figures. "These are the codenames they gave themselves as children, so her parents wouldn't know who she was spending time with. Amadi was the one who wrote the story you found in the library."

"He was the one who found me? The one who dragged me into the bliss pool?"

"Yes. After my mother died, he began to weaken. The fact that he lasted for so many years was a testament to his strength. The death of a parallel is debilitating. My mother's daimon searched all the worlds to find someone who would be a match to his daimon."

My eyes light up with understanding. "You have his daimon?"

"And you have my mother's dragon."

Her head drops onto my chest again. "I was so willful, so determined to be a dragon that I antagonized my own daimon —twice. I almost missed you because of stubbornness."

I rest my chin on the top of her head. We're already as close as is possible to be, but again I long to fuse ourselves together.

"I think you can get your wish then," I whisper.

"What's that?"

"That story—we can give it a happier ending."

She tips her head up, and I capture her lips. A gentle groan escapes her, rumbling through my chest as we press together.

She's warm and soft, and the taste of her has invaded my blood. Urgency hits me then, urgency and need. Her movements become frantic as well. We stumble over to the cot and topple onto it; even the small storm of dust that rises, disturbed from its resting place, doesn't distract us.

She pulls at my shirt. I stop kissing her long enough to pull it over my head, then help her out of hers. Within seconds, we're both in our underwear. I skate my fingertips over her curves, the swell of her breasts, the flare of her hips. Then follow with lips and tongue, tasting her skin, inhaling her scent, damn near losing my mind.

I meet her lips again, our mouths a frenzy. She rubs her hands up and down my chest, fingertips lingering on my scars. Then she pulls away to kiss them.

When she brushes over my heart, I press her hand to my skin firmly. "You know this is it forever, right? We're linked. It's like I can feel your souls."

"You're mine," she says simply.

"Forever."

Is this crazy? My mind is totally blown. But how is it any

crazier than me being brought from my deathbed through a portal to this carnival mirror version of the world?

All thoughts fly from my head as Celena pushes me back onto the bed. I go willingly, mouth hanging open as she climbs up to straddle me.

She looks like an angel above me, hair haloed in the light from the lantern. Then she lowers herself onto me, pressing the V of her legs onto my cock, though our underwear still separates us.

My hips jut up instinctively. I grab her waist. She chuckles, leaning down to kiss me. It takes some maneuvering since this cot wasn't built for two, but I roll us over so I'm on top. Position myself between her spread thighs and slip a finger inside her underwear. She's soaked.

Her lips part as I slide through her folds. Her eyes flutter closed.

"Victor," she whispers, all breathy. Her legs tremble and mine aren't exactly steady, either.

"It's all right if you're not ready," I say.

"It's not that, I just…haven't before."

I nod, understanding. Sheltered princess and all. "Are you absolutely sure you want to?"

Her eyes blink open and the look she gives me leaves no room for uncertainty. "Absolutely."

There are no condoms here, maybe not in this world at all, and a thought hits me—what would a baby with Celena be like? I decide it would be wonderful and slide my drawers down my legs. She shimmies out of her panties, and I notch myself at her entrance.

Her face goes slack as I slide into her slick heat. I bite off a groan. She gasps in a breath, and the tight fit strangling my dick makes my arms shake. I'm keeping all my weight off her, but I feel I might collapse at any moment, she feels so good.

Heat sparks up my spine. Sweat slicks my back. I wedge myself inside her slowly, not wanting to cause her any pain.

Celena wraps her legs around me and shifts her hips to accommodate my size. Her arms come around my back and the bite of fingernails score my back.

"Everything okay?" I ask.

"More than okay," she says, and I can breathe again. Then she rolls her hips, and I'm lost. We set a gentle rhythm that becomes frantic as heat and pleasure rise.

Her scent, her sweetness, the softness of her skin, the feel of her gripping me as I slide in and out. It's all overwhelming.

Sweat covers my skin as I focus on making it good for her, doing everything I can to hold out since it's been quite a while for me. Judging by the way she's attacking my back and clenching her thighs together, she's flying high. My eyes roll back in my head as her back bows off the thin mattress.

I reach for her clit, stroking gently, then pinching it softly, and she falls apart. As she shouts my name, her head shoots back. I let myself let go, giving over to the waves of pleasure that take me under, but having the presence of mind to pull out and spill onto her thighs.

Our heavy breathing fills the silence of the tiny room. I crush Celena in my arms, holding the woman who I took captive and now have fallen in love with.

THIRTY

Celena
_____

I COULD LIE in Victor's arms forever, but though we've been granted a brief respite from the approaching terror—an impossible to beat army set to destroy everything I've ever known—it won't last forever. Even now, I can feel the massive horde of Revokers regrouping.

"Why do you think they stopped?" I ask Victor, my voice trembling with anxiety. He knows exactly what I'm talking about.

"I think they sensed you and your daimon. They know that together as parallels we can end them forever."

Victor strokes his fingers up and down my shoulder. We're still squeezed onto this tiny cot together. If I had my way, we'd never leave. We'd live the rest of our lives in this room, smaller than my closet was in my suite inside the Citadel.

Now that my memories have returned, I understand everything that has been lost. The only home I've ever known, the place I was born, is now just a hole in the ground.

And my father gone as well. Though our relationship was difficult, though I never felt truly seen and heard, in his own way, he was always there for me, always believing in me.

He was my fiercest defender, never once showing doubt

that I could achieve whatever I put my mind to. I love him and miss him, but at the same time, I'm glad he's gone. There isn't really time to unpack the guilt and shame that comes along with those competing feelings.

"We need to go back," I say into the quiet.

"We do," Victor replies, his tone filled with regret. "Do you know what it will take to destroy the Revokers?"

"Unfortunately, yes. My mother told me. I think her great shame was not having the courage to do it herself." I sigh deeply, and though I relish the feel of my skin against his, I force myself to leave this nest of comfort, warmth, and love. Victor groans and rises as well. We dress silently.

"What do you think we should do?" he asks. "We have to tell them, right? It's going to change the future of both clans forever."

Dread coats my skin as I tie the laces of my boots. "Yes, it will. We need to find a way to alert both clans together. I don't want the fragile peace they've managed to create to be impacted by the news." I'm not looking forward to the reaction of either group. But as long as they don't blame each other and fall back into war, perhaps it will be all right.

Victor and I share a glance full of apprehension. He wants to do this as little as I do.

"How long do you think we have?" I ask. "Until the Revoker army is ready to move on us again?"

He strokes his chin, tilting his head to the side as if he's listening to something that I can't hear. The monsters have been inside his head for a dozen years; I've only been able to sense them for a handful of hours, so I trust his intuition about what they feel and want.

"Not long. I'm pretty sure they're just regrouping, but there's no way they're going to change what they want. They're still planning to tear down that wall and hunt us to extinction."

My mother's voice echoes back to me the way she sounded

in the Origin. She and the man she loved could have ended this all years ago, but they didn't. I understand why—the idea of such a sacrifice is chilling. Am I strong enough to do what she couldn't?

We step out into the afternoon light, saying a silent goodbye to our temporary shelter. That little room, which has held more than its share of heartache and longing, will always live in my memory, even if I never step foot inside its walls again.

Victor squeezes my hand gently, then steps far enough away to shift freely into the black dragon. I allow my daimon to change my body as well, and then we take to the sky.

He leads the way this time, but instead of going straight north, he leads me northwest to where the terrifying sight of thousands upon thousands of Revokers gathers.

They're oddly still, as if waiting for something. Then, in unison, they all look up. A sea of red eyes in black, scaled reptilian faces all staring my way, makes my heart go cold.

Their numbers are apocalyptic. They will wipe out every living thing in the city of Aurum if we don't stop them. But the only way to do that is to end life as we have always known it.

THIRTY-ONE

Celena

WE SOAR BACK UP to the wall, noting the short distance the Revoker horde must cross to be right on our doorstep. Down on the ground, workers hurry to patch the two full breaches, and on the southern side of the barrier, an entire army squadron protects those working to fill in the half-dozen openings left unfinished by the enemy.

Zanna is among their number. I land and shift to ask her where we can find Shad.

"He's in an emergency meeting," she snaps, appearing annoyed at the interruption. However, I'm starting to believe this moodiness is just her manner and not necessarily a reflection of her opinion of me. She reminds me a bit of Dominga in that way—a frosty exterior that protects a core of pure loyalty.

Zanna purses her lips. "He would have invited you, you know. If you'd been around. It's the type of thing you should probably be attending." However, she won't say more than that. She just gives me directions on where to find him, then re-focuses on her duties.

I don't have the heart to tell her that none of this labor to patch up the wall will matter. If that army gets here, the thick concrete might as well be matchsticks for all the good it will do.

Instead, I shift once more and join Victor in the sky, then we follow the route she gave me. It leads us north of the decaying city, across the water, to a solitary rocky island on the horizon.

Steep, jagged cliffs make up its desolate coastline as if nature sculpted this place with angry hands. The ruins of a large, pale building on top of the island are just a crumpled heap of concrete and steel. Wild vegetation exercises its superiority, vines and shrubs taking over what once must have been an imposing structure.

Several boats are tethered to a newly repaired dock, and on the top of a rise once accessible via a set of steps built into the ridge, a meeting takes place. The medley of people who have gathered was once unimaginable.

Shad is seated on a low boulder next to a handful of Nimali council members. Guards in their black uniforms stand watchfully behind him, along with several Cardinal advisors.

Across the table from them are four Fai men and women, who I imagine are their rulers—the Crowns of their Court. All are dressed elaborately in beautiful regalia with unusual jewelry encircling their wrists, necks, and in some of their hair. They also have a small group of guards and advisors hovering behind them.

The last group of people seated in the circle is even more surprising. They are not Nimali, and judging by their threadbare, well-patched but still ragged clothing, I can't picture them as Fai, either. Could they be human?

Victor and I set down a short ways away. The Fai and humans tense at our arrival. Several of the guards standing behind the Crowns call their daimons and glare at us with bright blue eyes. Shad's voice is carried away by the wind, but he must reassure them, for everyone calms as we shift forms.

"I see Alcatraz didn't make it through the Sorrows," Victor mutters.

Shad stands, then everyone in the circle does as well, with varying degrees of shock clear in their expressions. The Nimali present bow at me. Dominga is among their number, standing near the back of the group.

Her brows rise, but whether because of my daimon form or some other reason, I'm not sure. My best friend's expressions are well known to me, but she's too far away for me to determine if she's truly annoyed, amused-annoyed, or merely surprised.

"Princess Celena," Shad says, ushering me forward. "Victor." He gives my parallel a respectful nod. "May I present to you the Trivium." He sweeps an arm toward the circle, motioning toward all those present.

I approach, and one of our council members, Lady Raina, the youngest, offers me her seat. She was the same one who accused me of arriving in Aurum with an army of Revokers. Now, it seems, she wants to curry my favor.

Once, I would have considered the strategy of accepting her offer, or whether by not accepting I would send a stronger message of displeasure and leave her scrambling and unsettled. However, today, I'm wearied and so I sit. Victor stands behind me, a solid and comforting presence at my back.

"And what is the Trivium?" I ask.

"If I may, Your Majesty?" the silver-haired Fai woman asks. Shad inclines his head. The woman is clad in blue with an impressive amount of jewelry wound around her. Bright gray eyes peer at me from her deeply lined, tawny brown face.

"Princess Celena, we are gratified that you have returned safely. I am Water Priestess Citlali, First Crown of the Fai Court. The Trivium is an ancient order, an assembly of the Fai, human, and Nimali that existed in some parts of the world where humans were aware of our existence."

The group of humans watch, sharp-eyed. Staring is rude,

but I haven't ever been so near a human before. There are very few left in the city, and, of course, their paths would never cross a princess's.

My curiosity about them and how they live spikes. Without bliss, how does their society function? It's a question that's really never occurred to me before, but has suddenly become vital.

"King Shad learned of the historical existence of the Trivium," the water priestess continues, "and re-instituted it. Our current struggles mean that working together, both clans plus the various human tribes, is more important than ever before."

As she continues speaking of the newly re-formed collective, I'm awed to learn what Shad has managed to do in just a few short weeks of rule. Any doubts I may have harbored as to his suitability as king dissolve.

I don't believe I would have been able to bring these three groups together in the way that he has. And while the Citadel was destroyed on his watch, it might well have occurred if I were queen as well.

Moreover, I have no doubt the same Cardinals who oppose Shad's rule because of his Umber background only support me because they believe I would be easy to manipulate and use, whether I have a dragon daimon or not.

Shad's accomplishments are nothing less than miraculous. He is truly the king our people need in these dark times— there is no way I can lay the weight of what Victor and I must do at his feet.

As king, Shad stands poised to unite three factions who have been at odds since time immemorial. And he must have every chance to succeed. He needs the love and trust of our people, and the respect of everyone in this circle.

Something my father taught me comes to me at this moment. *If you want people who do not get along to do something together, you must give them a common enemy.*

While I never agreed with my father's cruel and barbaric methods, he was a masterful tactician, and I learned much at his feet. He would often set two parties against each other, on purpose, then unite them against a third party who may have something both of them wanted.

These games of influence and maneuvering were power plays for him. But even though he did not use the techniques for a noble purpose, they were effective.

Giving people someone to hate brings them together as much as giving them someone to love does. And light is only valuable because of the darkness.

The Revokers are a common enemy with enough might to wipe out all three of our groups. We must stand united against them in order to survive. However, if Victor and I are able to stop them, with the threat gone, there's a chance Nimali and Fai will start up their conflict again. Achieving true, lasting peace will require a sacrifice.

Suddenly, I understand what it means to be the queen who is needed. And that it is not necessarily the same as the queen who is loved.

I look over my shoulder at Victor, communicating with him silently, asking him with my eyes to follow my lead. The crinkling of his forehead indicates confusion, but there's trust in his gaze, and he nods at me.

I turn back. "I cannot tell you how impressed and shocked I am to find this gathering. It could not have come at a more important time. Have you sent out scouts? Have you seen the Revoker force that approaches?"

Grim faces meet me, along with solemn acknowledgment. They know the threat we face.

"All of you are witnesses to the fact that Victor and I have unique daimons. They are called Sentinels and have the ability to destroy the Revokers. All of the Revokers."

For a moment, there is silent disbelief. Then it becomes audible.

"How is this possible?"

"How can you know for sure?"

"Why should we believe that?"

I raise my hand, quieting their inquiries. "You do not have to believe us. You will see when it is done. And afterwards…" I breathe deeply, gathering my courage. "After it is complete, life will look very different here for all of you. If there were another way, we would take it, but there is not."

"What aren't you telling us?" one of the Fai rulers asks, an elderly man with pale skin wearing a yellow robe.

The faces gathered here are taut with tension. Fear and resignation are barely able to be pierced by hope. I'm more certain than ever that not telling them is the right thing.

"I think it is better if no one in this meeting knows. You can tell your people honestly that you had no idea. You can paint us as the villains. It will help stabilize things in the aftermath."

I turn to glance at Dominga; her brows are drawn together in concern. Feeling my heart crack open, I spin back around.

"One thing I learned from both my father and my mother is that being a ruler requires making difficult decisions. Impossible decisions, sometimes. And the people do not always thank you for it. But if we do not do this, everyone here will die."

Shad leans forward, trying to catch my eye, but I avoid him. My voice is too choked up to continue, so I stand. Victor places a hand on my shoulder, and it spreads needed warmth through my entire body.

"We have to go," I whisper. He wraps his hand around my waist and leads me away.

Voices rise with questions and alarm in our wake. Shad steps in front of us. "Celena?"

"Don't. I meant what I said. It's better if you don't know." I clear my throat so that I can continue. "I officially abdicate all claim to the Nimali throne. You are a good king, Shad. I have every faith in you."

Tears pool in my eyes, but Victor helps to keep me upright when I stumble getting around Shad. The expression on Shad's face is one of apprehension.

He knows what it cost me to do that.

The lump in my throat grows as we continue to walk. But then Dominga is in front of me, and my feet won't go another step.

Victor squeezes my waist.

"It's all right," I croak.

He steps away, back to the turmoil we've left behind us. Noise rises—more questions and confusion—but I shut it out, focused instead on my closest friend.

"What are you about to do?" Her voice is low, face placid as a calm sea while a storm rages in her eyes.

A sob escapes my chest, and I wrap my arms around her in a tight hug. "Thank you for always being there for me. You've been my greatest friend, and I'll never forget you."

"What are you about to do?" she repeats, wrapping her arms around me until they feel like comforting chains. "What is defeating them going to take?"

And because I've trusted her with everything since before I can remember, because I'm afraid I'll never see her again, and because she's the strongest person I've ever known, I tell her.

"We have to use the bliss. All of the bliss."

She pulls back, her dark brown eyes searching my face.

"The entire city will be bone dry, maybe the entire land—Nimali and Fai sources alike. There will be no more power, no more new daimons leashed."

She leans away from me, blinking rapidly. "Why?"

"I don't know. That's just what is required. The Sentinel daimons have additional abilities. They can draw strength from the bliss, but in order to have enough power to defeat every Revoker on its way here, they need every last drop of energy we can give them."

Her mouth closes with a snap, and I can practically see the gears turning in her head. She's running through ways to try and stop me, but it's half-hearted at best. I would never do something so drastic if it wasn't absolutely necessary.

Dominga's gaze shoots over to Victor then back to me. Her jaw trembles, her composure threatening to crack. "All right. If that's the only way for us all to survive. Fine. Do what you have to do." Then she spins on her heel and marches off.

Footsteps crunch over the rocky ground, and I feel Victor at my back. "You told her?"

"She won't tell."

We kicked over a hornet's nest here. Questions, concerns, doubts, worries, and fear radiate out from the meeting we crashed.

But in the end, it doesn't matter. The choice is between total annihilation and the end of life as we knew it. No more technology powered by bliss, no more peaceful pools of the blue liquid. And no more trials. No more daimons for those becoming adults. No more shifting.

Am I dooming my clan to extinction? Both clans? But we're both doomed already if I do nothing.

Heartsick and unable to keep what limited composure I have for any longer, I step far enough away from Victor to shift, and then launch into the air.

It's time to end this.

THIRTY-TWO

Victor
___

Leaving the island is a somber affair. A weight of uneasiness sits on the center of my chest. Celena and I can't talk in our shifted forms, and it's just as well—I don't even know what I would say. But I can feel her inside of me. Her sadness pulses like an extra heart.

We keep pace with each other, cruising over the length of the city once again. From the air, the landscape below is so desolate. Based on what I've pieced together overhearing the soldiers, the Nimali have spent decades repairing the buildings in their section of the city.

They live a fairly modern life that I'd recognize, re-engineering cars and trucks to not require gas, building computers and tablets I don't think I'd ever understand how to use, and those odd 3D video phones, which are honestly pretty cool. But all of it is powered by bliss. In the middle of the apocalypse, they've created technology and life, and we're taking that away from them.

To the west, the Fai settlement is hidden by the massive forest spreading out from what was once Golden Gate Park, through the Sunset District, and beyond. It's amazing to see how nature has reclaimed the urban landscape. But while the

Fai don't use bliss for energy, it's apparently an important part of their religion in ways I don't understand.

What will they all do without it?

Celena and I zoom past the wall, where the workers are still rushing to fix the damage. I fly low enough to spot Zanna. She tilts her head back, spotting us, her brow furrowed, and then we leave them all behind.

There's an area in the back of my head, near where it meets my neck, that tingles with the sense of the Revoker horde. They've grown agitated once more.

They're not on the move just yet, but as we draw closer to their position, my awareness of them sharpens.

My mind is full of traffic: there's my daimon's emotions, Celena's faint but growing presence, these creatures with their turbulent desires. I feel more than a little schizophrenic.

I drift down to the ground and settle on the barren soil about a hundred yards away from the wall of reptilian bodies. They're just standing there, so motionless it's actually eerie.

Celena settles next to me, the shiny black coat of her alicorn so beautiful even in the muted light of the overcast afternoon. The sun is going to set soon; I don't want to have to do this in the dark.

I stay shifted to maximize my connection to the Revokers, though I'm not under any illusions that I can control this many. It's impossible. But my awareness of them is extremely acute, and I'm sure I'll need every advantage.

"What do we need to do?" I ask the spirit inside of me.

It can't speak to me in words but sends feelings that are almost as vivid as images. A cool, calming sensation washes over me, reminding me of the bliss. It's relaxing, but at the same time, it wires me with an intensity that's almost frightening. It's as though I drank ten energy drinks in a row and am vibrating with the need for action.

My daimon gently presses me back, taking the reins of control of the dragon. I yield, relegating myself to the passenger seat for the first time since the spirit joined me all those years ago. It's strange being a witness and not the driver. But when the daimon fills the space I left behind, it's as if it puts on a perfectly fitted suit, one that I was just borrowing and was always a little baggy on me.

Now that I'm no longer in complete control, Celena's presence is even more intense. There's a bond, a delicate thread, that intertwines us, or maybe it intertwines our daimons—either way, the sensation mirrors the feeling of her nestled in my arms. The whispers of our connection run through me, offering strength.

I can also sense her daimon, another novel experience. The parallel link between my daimon and hers is like a feedback loop. The two share energy, which zips back and forth between them, growing with each pass, filling me up like a giant balloon.

And just when I think my mind is completely full—what with the spirits and princesses and monsters—there's something else, yet another presence. This one cool, smelling of frost, but also sweet and a little cloying like butterscotch sticking to the back of your tongue.

I'm trying to parse it out, separate all these energies and awarenesses within my mind, when suddenly, I'm in the Origin again. Or at least I think so. Everything around me is bright and white, like I've died and gone to heaven.

Celena is here as well. I can't see her or anything else, just the white light, but that sense of her being in my arms, even though I'm a bodyless spirit, stays the same, only now I can hear her voice.

"What's happening?" she asks.

"I have no idea," I reply. "Did our daimons bring us here?"

"I didn't think that was possible without being submerged in bliss."

"I don't think we know the half of what's possible with the Sentinel daimons."

"I suppose you're right," she says.

The presence of our daimons is visceral. Feeling them so strongly makes up for the lack of any other senses in this place. And because we're here, they can speak. Those strange, inhuman voices aren't really voices at all—more like words sent directly to your brain. But they're not talking to us. Celena and I are now just along for the ride.

"It is time," my daimon announces. The words echo inside me and all around at the same time. Purpose drives the Sentinels forward. It's clear in the tone of their speech.

A reply comes in the form of emotions firing at a rapid pace. They accompany that cool, sweet sensation that makes me all jittery and bombard me so quickly they're difficult to distinguish. I get a glancing sensation of stubbornness, exasperation, displeasure.

I'm reminded of trying to get my little sister to come inside when she'd been playing with her friends in the street and didn't want to go home. More than once, I had to physically drag her back while she pitched a tantrum—that is, until she got within sight of Ma, and quieted down real quick.

"It is time," my daimon says again, more forcefully. The emotions sent in reply are petulant, obstinate, but becoming resigned.

"I don't understand," Celena says.

"The bliss is a form of energy that exerts its will," her daimon responds. "It does not want to do what must be done; however, it will."

The idea that the bliss wants or doesn't want something hurts my brain. How is that even possible? Then again, I *am* floating without a body in a heavenly light source, being battered by the emotions of sentient blue goo. Nothing should freak me out at this point.

The bliss responds with longing and sorrow, wistfulness and apprehension. Worry.

"It is not forever," the two daimons say in unison. "But the Lost Ones must be dealt with. Then you may return to your games."

I get the distinct impression of parents cajoling and negotiating with a small child to eat their lima beans. In the end, they prevail, but it's not without a good amount of pouting.

Then, just as quickly as we were transported to the Origin, we're back in the real world. I'm once again tucked inside the body of the dragon, while my daimon holds the wheel.

Normally, when I shift into this form, it comes with additional energy and vitality—something I never questioned. Now, it's like we've gone from regular unleaded to rocket fuel. My energy points are off the charts.

If I were in control of the dragon, I don't think I'd be able to handle this much power. I've heard that driving a Lamborghini or some other super car is not like driving a Ford —not that I'll ever know. But people used to regular cars will drive an Aventador right off the road. It's just too much force beneath the hood for most to handle.

When I was a kid, I stuck a fork into the electric socket, probably just because Ma had warned me not to. I jumped at the surprise of it and the feeling of motorized ants crawling underneath my skin all at the same time. It was an aggressive tickle that really wasn't all that bad—though I never tried again. That experience is kind of like what normal levels of dragon power are like. Now, I'm pretty sure this is what it feels like to be struck by lightning.

Unimaginable power flows through me. That feedback loop between my daimon and Celena's? The power goes through that as well, swelling with each pass. I'm sure my hair would be standing on end if I was in my regular body.

Somehow, the Revokers sense what's going on. Where before they were still, now the wall of bodies snarls and thrashes. They are not happy campers. They're so unhappy, in fact, that they burst forward in a flurry of motion, rushing toward us. We're just two: a dragon and a winged unicorn facing off against an army of thousands.

The dragon opens its mouth and releases a deafening roar that echoes across the barren wasteland. That clicking in our chest starts up and flames shoot out of our mouth.

The flood of fire is accompanied by a wave of energy, one that originates within the dragon but quickly ripples across the distance to cover the Revokers. It stops the creatures in their tracks.

In just a few seconds, they managed to cross the football field length that separated us. Now, they're frozen. Every single one motionless, caught in the blast of energy shot forward by my daimon.

This power coursing through us, courtesy of the bliss, is mind-blowing. With each passing second, it surges through our veins, back and forth between my daimon and Celena's, igniting a euphoric rush that tingles with electric intensity. The air crackles with an unseen energy, and for a brief moment, invincibility surges within me.

But as the energy swells, the bliss wanes.

The amount needed to fuel us in this stand against the Revokers is drawing down the supply of bliss from within the city.

An undercurrent of concern tugs at my daimon, followed by a jolt of surprise, then fear. Though I don't know its thoughts, what I sense from all these connections I maintain makes it clear.

The bliss is running out quickly. Probably faster than anyone thought.

Even using all of it might not be enough.

THIRTY-THREE

Celena

BOTH MY DAIMON and Victor's strain while holding back the tide of the Revokers. Our spirits' increasing worry leaves me cold and shivering inside my mind.

"What do you need?" I scream mentally, wanting to help in some way but being unable to.

I don't expect a response—they can't speak to us in words outside of the Origin, but I do hear something. A word spoken so quietly, it might just be my imagination. "More."

More what? More power? More bliss? The bliss pours its bright, crackling energy into us, but the problem has always been, once it's gone, it's gone.

Twenty-five years ago, when my mother and the man she loved first joined with their daimons, the amount of bliss in this city was orders of magnitude higher. And there were far fewer Revokers.

If she had had the courage…but I can't think ill of her. I can't second-guess her choices because I wasn't there to make them. And I've made enough mistakes of my own.

At the moment, our efforts are holding back the Revoker army, but it's exhausting. Though my daimon took control of this body and I gladly let it, not knowing what to do, I still feel the strain. The gradual weakening.

Moreover, the spirits' fear bleeds into me. I'm sure this is not what they had hoped for. If we can't hold the Revokers, we'll be destroyed by them, along with everyone else.

My first thought is of Victor. And how, the last time you see someone, you don't know it will be the last. Did I ever tell him I love him? Did I say the words aloud and not just assume he understood because our souls are now connected?

Regrets, so many regrets, pass through me. So many things I should have done differently.

I reach out to him mentally, hoping he will somehow hear and understand, and maybe we'll see each other in the Origin again. I can tell him then.

Overhead, a fluttering sound catches my attention. Curiosity seizes my daimon as well. We raise our head and look up to an unexpected sight: a green dragon soaring alone in the sky. No, it's not alone; a man flies next to it, his incandescent blue eyes cutting through the gloom of the failing afternoon.

My heart seizes as Talia and Ryin land next to us. I jolt as a surge of power pushes through the loop that Victor and my daimons created. Somehow, Talia and Ryin are feeding us energy. How is that possible?

Our exhaustion and strain recede a fraction. Tiny cracks and fissures in our defense are being patched, just by the presence of the newcomers. Even as the bliss is nearly exhausted, we're holding steady. Holding strong.

More flapping sounds overhead, and the enormous blue dragon arrows toward us. He moves gracefully through the air to land nearby with an earth-shaking vibration. On his back rides the Fai woman he's betrothed to, Xipporah. She leaps down with feline grace, her daimon called and ready.

Another, smaller creature races down Shad's leg, though she is not exactly small. This is a different kind of dragon—

one who is nearly eight feet long, with a thin, forked tongue snapping out to test the air. The Komodo dragon shifter stays in her daimon form, her long, heavy tail flicking slowly back and forth. Dominga.

After her successful daimon trial, we joked that one day we would both be dragons. Now, Dominga's claws scrabble over the hard-packed ground, while my alicorn dances on sturdy hooves, excitement building.

With the arrival of each new daimon and host, more and more energy feeds into our bond. Victor's daimon uses it to bolster the energy field, keeping the Revokers from attacking us.

However, the creatures have broken free of the power that froze them in place. They can't move closer to us, but they writhe and churn. Scream out in anger and aggression and—I hope this is not just wishful thinking—a tinge of fear.

The alicorn turns its head to spot more and more Nimali and Fai arriving. Winged creatures and those in human form whip through the air. On the ground, the land forces of both clans run toward us.

Ryin steps to our side. "Those with Water daimons wait in the ocean in case they are needed," he says, motioning with his head toward the shore, not visible from where we stand, but not far away.

I long to ask him if Dominga revealed our plans after all—she must have—but no one seems to be here to stop us. Instead, they're joining us in making this stand. Even if I were not currently just a consciousness tucked into my daimon's form, my throat would be too choked up to speak.

With the arrival of more daimons, the power feedback loop between me and Victor strengthens, as does the containment of the Revokers.

Relief, excitement, and resolve shoot to me from Victor's end. Whether it's from him or his daimon or both, I'm not sure. But it charges my own emotions and those of the spirit I share this body with.

I sense the moment that his plan changes.

Victor's dragon spreads his wings and rises into the air; my alicorn follows. Behind us, stretching all the way back to the wall, the convergence of Fai and Nimali expands.

Even so, our numbers are nowhere near as large as the enemy gathered in front of us. However, every single daimon spirit contributes their energy. Their connection to the Origin fuels them, the same way as it does the bliss. It strengthens us, adding little by little to the reserve of power that lets us finally go from defense to offense.

The intent of our daimons becomes clear to me at last. They want to push the Revokers into the sea.

Victor and I fly in repeating arcs, pressing forward that energy shield and herding the Revokers to the west. The going is excruciatingly slow. But as we lead the way, the others catch on to our plan.

Fai shout orders, announcing that we're going to flank the Revokers and push them to the water. It's well known that the creatures cannot go underground or over water—we will use their weakness against them.

A handful of miles separate us from the seashore. Every step we take draws deeper from the well of energy, but the presence of the others, all the others, keeps us going. And as we get closer, the energy from the Water daimons flows into us as well, joining the loop, keeping us from flagging.

Within the barrier we created, the Revokers rage and roar. Their noise grows deafening as the water finally comes into view. They renew their attack against the shield of power, pummeling it with all their strength.

I don't know how we withstand it, but the presence of both clans working together for our common survival seems to be enough to make it happen.

There is no calm beach here with waves lapping at the

shore. A jagged, rocky cliff separates the land from the water, as if a large chunk of earth fell away, probably during the Sorrows. Collectively, we press and push the Revokers right to the edge of the cliff.

The first row falls into the water, accompanied by screams and splashes. The alicorn flies ahead to monitor.

As soon as the dark reptilian bodies hit the frothing waves, they dissolve, leaving behind only the bones of the bodies they stole.

It's a horrific and terrifying sight, but one that also gives hope. These creatures will not be returning.

In the water, a perimeter is formed by whales and dolphins, fish, crabs, octopuses, and a host of other sea creatures, including a kraken, as well as the Fai embodying all of the above within their human bodies. I glimpse the Water Priestess herself moving through the waves with ease, eyes shining in the growing dusk.

Together, those on land, air, and sea form a circle that completely surrounds the Revokers, squeezing them into a tighter and tighter configuration.

We push the army over the cliff and into the water, inch by inch, foot by foot, until the ocean is just a graveyard. It may be macabre, but it's the only way to thwart their plan of wiping out all life.

I don't know how long it takes, but the sun sets and the moon rises, and we push on and on, until there are none left.

THIRTY-FOUR

Celena

I STAND on the edge of the cliff overlooking the ocean. The light of a nearly full moon reflects off the blackness of the water like a mirror. The waves are calm and peaceful now, bearing no hint of the carnage falling to the ocean's floor.

Some sense within me recognizes my best friend a few seconds before she arrives at my side. "You told them." There's accusation in my voice, but no anger.

"I did what had to be done." Dominga's voice is icy, her emotions as tightly controlled as ever. "You always think you have to go at everything alone. I hope one day you understand that isn't true."

I reach out to grab her hand, gripping it tight. "Thank you."

She shrugs. "Thank Xipporah. Land Fai have some kind of connection to the bliss. They can also recharge the power of others. She's the one who figured out that gathering everyone together would strengthen whatever it is you all were trying to do. And thank the Origin we didn't have to hold hands to do it. That would have been a step too far." She squeezes my hand as punctuation.

Behind us, a celebration rages. Fai and Nimali gather,

reliving the day's events, their voices filled with wonder. They sit around fires and cluster in groups, crossing divides that are generations deep.

It's done. The Revokers gone forever. And I'm glad for it. I just worry that tonight's joy will morph into tomorrow's despair. I don't think the people know exactly what has been lost yet. They will soon find out the very foundation of the lives of both clans is about to change dramatically.

"We created a life out of nothing once," Dominga says, reading my thoughts. "We can do it again. And I suppose being on good terms with the barbaric Fai, learning their techniques for living without bliss, will come in handy." Her voice is wry, but she speaks the truth.

"Humans, too," I add. "They've been surviving right alongside us, with no magic and even fewer resources."

She hums in response, never taking her eyes off the water. "Akeem reports that the library remains intact."

I turn at that, brows raised. "Really?"

She nods, still focused on the dark expanse of the ocean. "Apparently, every drop of bliss in the city, except for the tanks below the library that hold all of our knowledge, is gone. No one else knows, though, just Shad. Now you."

I'm pretty sure Shad didn't share this information with her. However, Dominga has always made it her business to know what no one else does.

My gaze skates across the groups of people that a few weeks ago would never have been caught dead helping each other. We fought and killed, captured and enslaved, hated and feared one another. Even in my wildest secret dreams of becoming queen and making positive change, I couldn't have imagined the sight before me, nor what we accomplished today ever being possible.

From a few feet away, Victor watches us. Though Dominga can't possibly see where I'm looking, she says, "You love him?"

I still haven't said those words aloud to him, so instead of agreeing, I say, "He is mine, and I am his."

She pulls her hand out of mine and crosses her arms. Then finally looks me in the eye. "Good. Maybe now you'll figure out that being alone is not always best."

Her voice cracks. I look at her sharply.

"Dominga—"

She shakes her head, holding up a hand. "I don't believe in goodbyes." And then she's walking away. I want to call her back, but the set of her shoulders is so severe that I don't.

Is this goodbye? She's always seen and known more than me. I silently hope she will take her own advice and allow someone to pierce her hard, brittle shell. Though I know her better than anyone else, in many ways, she's still a mystery. An island unto herself.

My eyes sting as I watch her head along the cliff's edge, back straight, head up, but feeling the same pain that I do. I owe her so much that I can never repay. That she'd never even let me.

Then Victor is there. I inhale his scent and lean against the tall strength of him. He wraps his arms around me, and it's like he's touching every part of me. All three of my souls.

"Do you feel it?" he asks.

I don't have to ask him for clarification because I do feel it. Within me, my daimon is restless. It has done what it came here to do. The Sentinels are not like the other daimons. They have no desire to exist within us, witnessing the material world, living for as long as their hosts live, content to sit in the passenger seat.

Sentinels are active. Without a threat to rail against, they have no purpose.

"What are we supposed to do?" I whisper.

Victor doesn't respond.

We hover at the edge of things for the rest of the night

until the celebrants eventually make their way back north to homes or tents or the arena filled with refugees.

Finally, when the glow of dawn crests upon the horizon, the only ones left are Shad, Xipporah, Talia, and Ryin. Victor and I approach the place where they sit sleepily staring into the remnants of a dying fire.

My mood is grim. I largely stayed away from the celebration, having no desire to dim the joy of others. But these four know exactly what kind of road they'll be walking in the coming days, months, and years. They know how hard it will be.

"I think it is better if we leave," I say. "Head back to the city across the water. That way, the people will have someone to rage against."

Shad stands, shaking his head. "This is not about blame. There is no reason we cannot move forward together."

I draw myself up, pushing the words out. "Even though I've abdicated, there still will be those who try to sow seeds of doubt and division. My presence here cannot help you anymore."

His lips firm. He can't gainsay me because he knows I'm right.

I don't bother to tell them about our daimons. About how I'm almost certain they're preparing to abandon us. Soon, Victor and I will be mundane humans, and to be so here would mean being confronted by everything I've lost at every moment for the rest of my life.

I've gained a lot, too, and I have no regrets, but I would rather face the unknown future at Victor's side, content that my absence will help my people.

They all protest further, but my mind is made up. I believe that Victor would be fine with staying if that is what I wanted, but he's happy to follow my lead in this. His emotions still pulse within me.

When we lose our daimons, we'll lose that bond, something I will regret. But I know the parallel link is not the only thing, or even the strongest thing, tying us together.

"Whether or not you choose to blame us for the missing bliss is for you to decide," I tell Shad. "Perhaps the Trivium can vote on it. But we cannot stay."

Concern is etched on his face, drawing down the corners of his eyes and mouth. "I understand. This will always be your home, Celena. And you will be welcomed back should you ever choose to return."

He bows to me, solemnly, and I thank him.

I turn to face Talia, who has tears in her eyes. "Thank you for your assistance. I am in your debt and regret that I will not be able to repay it."

Her lips quirk. "No, I was in your debt. I stole your life for a while and made a mess of it. Consider us even." Then she rushes forward and wraps me in her arms, squeezing me tight.

It's unexpected and I freeze for a moment, before hugging her back. Thoughts of what type of person I would be if I had grown up in her world pepper me. I know nothing of her history, and now will forever remain ignorant.

Victor and Ryin share quiet words. I nod respectfully at Xipporah, who will take my place as queen. A Fai queen is exactly what is needed now for the future ahead. And I'm certain that if Shad and his daimon chose her, she is up to the task.

Once we've said our final goodbyes, Victor and I take to the air. Perhaps for the last time.

We slip through the darkness, though my daimon is able to see in low light. I focus on the feel of air beneath my wings. Of floating on the current, and the coiled strength in my limbs.

I expect Victor to head east, across the water, to his tower, his gardens and murals and library. But instead, he flies north, to the Nimali sector of the city. My home for all of my life.

He sets down on the grassy plaza that formed the center

of my clan's life. The Citadel once stood at its edge. Now, the grand building that represented the strength of the Nimali is just a gigantic crater in the earth.

Did he believe I needed to see it one last time?

Still in my alicorn form, I walk up the very edge of the pit and stare into the darkness of the abyss. The emotions that pass through me are something of a surprise. There is some grief, remorse for all those who lived here who have lost everything, but not as much pain as I would have thought.

The Citadel could not have functioned in the new world the Nimali are stepping into. No one could live in such a building without any bliss to power the lights, elevators, heating and cooling, and a dozen other things.

All the things I once thought were so important are gone, and I don't even miss them. I feel like a totally different woman from the one who left here in the middle of the night all those weeks ago intent upon leashing a daimon.

"One of these buildings is the library, isn't it?" Victor asks from behind me.

I shift so we can speak and point it out. The swooping silver lines of its unique architecture glint in the rising dawn light.

"There's something I want to ask my daimon before we go. Would you be okay with one more trip to the Origin?"

I hadn't thought he was standing close enough to overhear Dominga mention the library and its remaining store of bliss, but apparently, he was. I agree and follow him into the building.

The vast space is several degrees cooler than outside, dimly lit by an ambient glow of bliss from an open floor panel. The bliss that holds all the data stored in the library is directly under the floor. When accessed via normal means, it shoots up into a spray that delivers information in images and audio.

Now it's just potential, a placid lake of liquid hidden

beneath this level of the building. The space is silent and Akeem, the librarian, is nowhere to be found.

Suddenly, I'm filled with gratitude that all of our knowledge has remained. The tanks under the floor hold so much information. The entire history of our clan, stories recorded and passed down through the generations, as well as knowledge of the world before the Sorrows, and so much more that I never bothered to uncover and learn about.

At least that will not be lost.

Victor slips into the liquid first. I slide in after him, and we are transported once more—for what will likely be the last time—to the Origin.

Our daimons greet us, their presence palpable, almost like a touch against my skin.

Victor speaks first. "You want to stay here, don't you?"

Both of our daimons reply with one voice. "Our task in the material world is complete. We have no wish to remain linked any longer. However, since you have been vessels for us, and have assisted us in completing our mission, we are able to offer you a choice."

I wonder if it will be the same choice my mother and father offered me, perhaps other daimons to replace the ones we're losing?

"Victor, we delivered you here without your consent and against your will. The need was great but we are not insensible of the injustice of it. Would you like to return to your world?"

Shock blanks out my thoughts for a moment. An earthquake shatters my equilibrium.

Victor's voice shakes when he answers. "Y-you can do that?"

"Indeed."

My mind is frozen. Fear snakes icy fingers through my consciousness. Victor can go home.

"And what about Celena?" he asks. "I'm not going anywhere without her."

Longing and regret and sorrow and love batter me, cutting through the frost. I cannot allow him to stay for me.

The daimons sound just a bit more human when they respond. "Both of you may go, if you wish it."

A sob escapes me. I wish I could see him. Touch him. Hold him.

"Celena...is that something you might want?" He sounds so unsure.

As soon as I have a body again, I intend to cling to him like a vine and never let go. Make sure he can feel in every way possible exactly what he means to me. Until then, I settle for making my voice as emphatic as possible. "There's nothing left for me here. I love you, Victor, and I'll go wherever you go. Whatever life brings us, we will face it together. You are the only one in all the worlds for me."

His voice stutters. "I...I love you, too, Celena. You know that the world I come from is very different than here. Are you totally sure? I can't offer you the life of a princess."

My souls smile. "You were forced to give up everything you'd ever known to save my world. I will gladly choose to do the same to be with you."

Our choice made, we thank our daimons and get ready for our next adventure.

Epilogue

THE LIBRARIAN ENTERS HIS DOMAIN, grateful that it still exists. In the days to come, he will, no doubt, be required to fight many of his people in order to keep the sanctity of the library intact. But today he can simply enjoy the quiet and the way the atmosphere of generations worth of knowledge feels against his skin.

He maneuvers his considerable bulk to push open a door that, before, would have slid open automatically. But he's not bothered by the effort; he rarely has to exert himself physically these days and doesn't mind the change of pace.

The staircase in this building was not originally built wide enough for his use. However, several days before it became necessary, he undertook a solo construction project to widen it, telling no one. Now that the elevator is no longer an option, he winds his way down the new stairs, grateful once more for the benefits that maintaining his daimon form at all times gives him. For the information that the librarian alone is privy to.

His destination is the bottom floor of the building, and a thick metal door that opens on creaking hinges indicating its infrequent usage. He has visited more in the past month than in all the years before combined.

The air is thick and warm, and a sense of vertigo spins his mind for a moment as he steps through the entrance. He once described this place as a portal, a location both here and there where the material world and the Origin exist together. There are very few of these zones left in the world.

The librarian moves to stand at the edge of the pit leading deep into the earth. Once, there was bliss here, its blue glow offering a little light. Now, pitch darkness surrounds him. He relies only on his prodigious memory of the place and its exact layout to keep from tumbling into the depths of the yawning cavity.

The bliss that once flowed below was taken back to the Origin and used to rid the material world of those called the Lost Ones. And while the clans still celebrate their victory over the Lost Ones, the librarian alone knows there were no defeats on that day.

While the Revokers did not achieve their goal of wiping out all life in the city, their ultimate aim was peace. As Fai, Nimali, and human leaders continue to share resources and aid one another, it cannot be said that the sacrifice of the Lost Ones was in vain.

In the Origin, where their daimons returned, even the old conflicts they waged with the others have quieted.

Staring down into the chasm that was once full of vibrant blue liquid, something other than sorrow fills him. The librarian waits and watches.

He is rewarded by a glimpse of another world in his mind's eye. A gift from the spirit within him.

There is a street, bearing houses whose windows are all filled with glass. Doors hang properly on their hinges. Lawns are neatly trimmed. Fully functioning vehicles in good repair sit parked on a street that is marred by occasional cracks and divots, but otherwise well-paved and maintained.

A familiar man stops at a mailbox attached to a fence, running his fingers over the letters forming his last name. He looks up to the house before him, a two-story structure painted in green with black shutters. Tears well in his eyes. His hand reaches out to grasp that of the woman he's with. Together, they slowly approach the porch.

The man knocks on the door, holding his breath. It's opened by an older woman who shares his facial shape and coloring. Her dark eyes widen with disbelief. When it looks as though she might swoon, the young man grabs her hands, keeping her upright, and says, "It's really me, Ma." Then he falls into her arms.

The woman with him, who once held one of the highest ranks in a powerful clan, looks on, love shining in her eyes. Soon they are all crying and hugging. Greeting one another.

The two newcomers ready themselves to tell an impossible tale, one that is nearly beyond belief.

And in that liminal place below the library, on the cusp of not just two worlds, but all the worlds, the librarian hears a soft trickle.

Down below, in the furthest reaches of a pit that stretches into the very heart of existence, a soft blue light emerges. Just a few drops for now. But in time…

The librarian smiles and turns away.

About the Author

L. Penelope has been writing since she could hold a pen and loves getting lost in the worlds in her head. She is an award-winning fantasy and paranormal romance author. Her novel *Song of Blood & Stone* was chosen as one of *TIME* Magazine's 100 Best Fantasy Books of All Time. Equally left and right-brained, she studied filmmaking and computer science in college and sometimes dreams in HTML. She hosts the *My Imaginary Friends* podcast, co-hosts the *Ink and Magic* podcast, and lives in Maryland with her feline dependents.

www.lpenelope.com
hello@lpenelope.com